The Trap

(An Agent Dallas Thriller)

by L.J. Sellers

Novels by L.J. Sellers

Detective Jackson Mysteries

The Sex Club

Secrets to Die For

Thrilled to Death

Passions of the Dead

Dying for Justice

Liars, Cheaters & Thieves

Rules of Crime

Crimes of Memory

Deadly Bonds

Wrongful Death

Agent Dallas Thrillers

The Trigger

The Target

The Trap

Standalone Thrillers

The Baby Thief

The Gauntlet Assassin

The Lethal Effect

THE TRAP

Cover art by Gwen Thomsen Rhoads

ISBN (ebook): 978-0-9840086-8-1
ISBN (print): 978-0-9840086-9-8
Published in the USA by Spellbinder Press

DEDICATION

The Agent Dallas series wouldn't be possible without the help of a team of professionals. I'm grateful for my editor, Jodie Renner, for helping me polish my stories and crank up the tension, and for my graphic artist, Gwen Rhoads, and her brilliant covers. I also deeply appreciate my proofreaders, Joan Huston and Barry Young, who find all my last-minute errors. And a special thanks to my superior ebook formatter, Kimberly Hitchens of Booknook.biz.

Chapter 1

Wednesday, Oct. 1, 10:05 a.m., Corona Arch, Utah
Jamie Dallas braced for the jump, pulling in a deep breath. She stood on a fifty-foot rock arch under a massive blue sky, and the exquisite autumn moment was about to get insanely better.

"Go already," Luke said. "Unless you're chickening out."

"Never." Dallas ran four steps and leapt off the rock into the thin air. Gravity yanked her down, and she tightened her grip on the cable. Free-falling! A rush of adrenaline pulsed through her body. The moment the rope hit its full extension, she leaned back and pumped her legs. Her body swung wildly under the arch, coming up on the other side. Glorious! She threw her weight back in the other direction and let out a wild cry of joy, followed by an exuberant body laugh. The world's biggest swing in the most beautiful setting. The closest she'd ever come to flying—except for hang gliding. Or maybe parasailing. But this was better, more out of control.

Above her on the rocks, her new friends—technically her targets—laughed and called for her to show them something. Dallas executed a series of aerial stunts, her body bursting with the joy of being upside-down, weightless, and in motion. *Damn!* This was good.

When the momentum died, Luke and Abby pulled her up.

Dallas stepped onto the solid rock and grinned. "That was incredible!" Another group of thrill-seekers sprawled on the nearby outcropping, waiting their turn.

Luke smiled back. "*You* were incredible. I loved those stunts."

These people were easy to like, and she had moments when she forgot she was an undercover agent, intent on sending them to prison. She'd been working the case for months, meeting up with the group in various locations around the country to hang glide or BASE jump or some other wild adventure.

She'd first met Luke and Abby in Vegas, when a group of fifty people had gathered to skydive for a video stunt they hoped would go viral. The weekend had been a personal adventure Dallas had signed up for online, a quick trip from her hometown. But after the jump, while packing her gear, she'd overheard snippets of the couple's conversation that made her FBI nerves jangle. The words *hack* and *sabotage* used closely together had to be about criminal enterprise, and *terminate* sounded like they had murder in mind.

She'd taken her concerns to her boss in the Phoenix field office, and he'd encouraged her to stay in touch with the couple through their shared thrill-sport passion. Out of habit from her job and a personal sense of fun, she'd used an alias to sign up for the original adventure, so her cover had been established from the beginning. After she learned Luke and Abby were prison-reform activists, the bureau had done the rest by creating a background for her that would appeal to the couple.

Dallas unbuckled her harness, and Luke high-fived her. "You rock. You're officially a Flyer." At five-nine, Luke wasn't much taller than her, but he was a bodybuilder with incredible strength, and his compelling face was blemished only by a weak chin.

"Hell yeah!" Dallas did a little happy dance. At twenty-eight, she was still allowed.

"I don't know how you get in and out of that safety harness so easily," Abby said. Luke's girlfriend was his opposite, with a long lean body and cropped dark hair that made her look even taller. Her delicate facial features bore the pockmarks of an earlier life of drugs, and her eyes held a lifetime of distrust.

Dallas recognized another opportunity to identify with the group and took it. "I was a skilled lock-pick in my early wild years. I can get into almost anything."

Luke laughed. "You never fail to surprise me."

"I like to keep it interesting." Dallas handed over the gear. She'd gone on several more adventures with the club, staying close to the couple and their friend Cree. Late-night drinking and gabbing sessions with the group had led her to believe they were targeting politicians who stood in the way of the reform they wanted. After a teleconference with FBI headquarters, the bureau had green-lighted a full undercover investigation, and she'd moved to an apartment in Washington DC to be near where the three lived.

They were also members of a national organization called Justice Reform Now (JRN), which was pushing to change drug and sentencing laws and improve prison conditions through legislation and social-media outreach. Her task was to infiltrate the secret inner circle and discover their agenda. The bureau had given them, and her undercover assignment, the code name Freeman. The activists knew her as Tara Adams, a ghostwriter with a criminal record turned political blogger. She'd kept her hair blond for this assignment, because they'd already seen her that way, but she'd started wearing dark eye makeup and green contacts to change her look. She was still waiting for Luke to ask her to join their cause.

"I can't wait to go again," she said, buckling Abby into the harness.

"We'll see if we have enough time." Luke caressed her arm, then leaned in and whispered, "You're so sexy when you're high on adrenaline."

More progress. This was the second time he'd shown a personal interest.

Abby's eyes sparked with jealousy. "What's the secret?"

Dallas smiled and laughed. "He thinks I'm crazy." She didn't want to alienate Luke's girlfriend, but to be successful in her assignment, she might have to. Being an undercover agent for the bureau allowed her to put her attractiveness to good use, and seduction was one of her specialties. She was also a sharpshooter, but that skill came in handy less often. Luke, the leader, was her main target, and earning his affection was the fastest way to get inside and find out what they were really up to.

Luke gave his girlfriend a one-armed hug of reassurance. "You ready to go for a swing?"

A pause while Abby locked eyes with Luke. "Don't do it." Abby turned and started for the edge of the arch.

Don't do what? Something was coming down and Abby was against it. Dallas pulled a beer from the cooler, high-fived Cree, and took a seat on a rock ledge. She kept to herself, hoping Luke would come and talk to her after Abby made the jump.

And he did. As Luke sat down, he asked, "If they make it illegal to play here, would you still do it?"

Dallas laughed. "Of course. The BASE jump we did last month was illegal. Morality and legality are not the same." She realized why he'd asked her, and a shiver of excitement ran up her spine. "I'm a natural-born rule-breaker."

"Most adrenaline-junkies are." Luke's smile disappeared. "Would you break the law to promote a political cause? I mean, if you had tried everything else and lives were at stake?"

Dallas chose her words carefully. "Within reason, yes. As long as innocent people didn't get hurt."

"Good to know. Especially since you share our passion for reforming the justice system."

The inner circle had talked politics with her at the last two adventures, drinking and discussing the issues long into the night. Luke was right about the unfairness of drug sentences and the horrific conditions inside prisons, so it had been easy to pretend to sympathize with his ideology. "Something has to change," Dallas said. "And it's never going to come from Congress."

Luke patted her leg. "I want you to come to a meeting Friday night. You've met most of the group already—me, Abby, and Cree—and we have one more member who doesn't come on our thrill trips."

"A political meeting?"

He nodded. "At our place southeast of Fairfax Station."

Yes! She was in. Dallas worried he would notice her escalating pulse and forced herself to sound casual. "Sure." The high school acting lessons her aunt had paid for, to keep her busy, had prepped Dallas well for this job. The political science courses in college had been a plus too, when she'd applied at the bureau.

Cree walked up, his long braid hanging over his shoulder.

"Hey, maybe we should offer Tara a ride back, since we're all going to DC." Cree glanced at Luke. A trust-fund kid with a rebel heart, Cree was a pilot with access to his family's plane. Dallas suspected he also helped fund their excursions.

"We can't," Luke said. "The plane is full."

Cree started to respond, then stopped.

Dallas got the feeling there was another reason Luke didn't want her along. Maybe a stop they had to make. "No problem," she said. "I've got a non-refundable return ticket anyway." She took a long pull of the cold beer, eager to contact her FBI team leader. "Where's the meeting?"

"I'll pick you up around five."

Luke didn't trust her enough yet to give her the address. She had no reason to give him hers. "I've got a busy day Friday, so I'll text you my location at around four."

He held up his bottle for a toast. "To our new level of friendship."

Dallas clinked beers with him. "I think I'm gonna like this."

Later, while waiting to catch her flight back to the capital, she dug into the secret compartment at the bottom of her backpack for her burner phone. This one was exclusively for reporting to Agent Drager, her undercover contact. Two additional agents were on her UC team, but she'd never met them. It was safer for her that way. And she'd only talked face-to-face with Drager once, at a brief clandestine encounter. Going anywhere near the FBI field office or being seen with an agent was too risky. The main JRN group had been operating in Washington DC for years, and Luke was a well-known activist with many connections.

Dallas texted Drager: *I'm in! Going to a house southeast*

Fairfax Station on Friday for meeting at five. No address yet. They're picking me up.

As she settled into her seat on the plane, Drager texted back: *Good job! Let's meet tomorrow for an update. Could be our last chance before they isolate you.*

The words gave her a chill. But that was how activist, cult-like groups functioned and kept members in line. She knew from experience in infiltrating a survivalist compound. She texted: *When and where?*

Drager came back with: *I'll contact you at noon. Be in the downtown area.*

The plane started to taxi, and Dallas turned off her phone. Her body was tired, but her brain wouldn't let her relax. Once she was a member of the inner circle, her contact with Drager would be limited. This could turn out to be her most dangerous assignment yet. She might have to participate in illegal activities to win their trust and gather enough evidence for a conviction. If the group found out she was a federal agent, they might kill her to protect themselves. Sometimes her job scared the hell out of her—but that was why she loved it.

Chapter 2

Wednesday, Oct. 1, 9:35 p.m., Emporia, Virginia

Luke Maddox hunched forward in his seat, watching the lights on the ground below. Despite his love for daredevil sports, landing made him nervous, especially in small aircraft. Cree was a good pilot, but he smoked a lot of late-night pot, and Luke never quite relaxed on their trips. But he was lucky to have Cree, and his family plane, supporting their missions. A wealthy donor who'd contacted him through JRN made their secret campaign possible. He or she preferred to remain anonymous and deposited monthly donations into a bank account Luke had opened under a charity name.

"Ree-lax," Cree said, drawing out the word. "We're almost down."

But Luke couldn't. He hated the southern part of Virginia and had sworn to never return. The rural airport below was less than fifty miles from the state prison where he'd wasted ten years of his life. He still couldn't think about it without tensing.

"Maybe you should sit back." Cree laughed. "You're not really a co-pilot, and you look like you're ready to jump."

That almost made him laugh. He'd met Cree two years ago during a skydiving event, so he *had* already bailed out of a plane his friend was piloting. "Sorry, you know I hate landing. That's why I prefer to jump." Abby, on the other hand, was sleeping soundly in the back.

Cree snorted and gave him a fist bump. "I hope Aaron is at the airport and ready to go. We're running late."

"He will be. Number crunchers like to be punctual." Aaron Foster had joined their group four months earlier, offering his analytical and tech skills to their cause after he'd been diagnosed with pulmonary fibrosis and knew his days were numbered. Facing early death had motivated Aaron to make his life count for something. Aaron's sister had died in prison, so the cause was personal for him too. They'd dropped off the analyst on their way to Utah so he could attend yet another family funeral.

"Hang on, we've got a little crosswind now." Cree's smooth baritone held a note of concern.

Luke closed his eyes. If he died today, he had no regrets about the last few years. He didn't consider himself a bad guy. The criminals were the politicians and judges who ruined lives with excessive and often-immoral punishments. Luke had just turned eighteen when he'd been arrested for possession of marijuana—plus intent to distribute—his first and only brush with the law. A typical teenager who'd experimented with pot. Yet, a conservative judge had sentenced him to ten years. Luke had done the full decade of his time—and emerged from prison a different person. The bitterness was part of him now. So was the stigma. He had no choice but to try to save others from the same fate.

He couldn't shake the memory. Ten years of his life caged like an animal. The beatings, the humiliation, the lack of sunlight were enough to break a man—but nothing compared to the depression. Waking every day and wondering if he would be better off dead. And for what? It had all started with his friend Ryan's older brother, who was a pot dealer. Ryan had pinched a small bag of pot from his brother's stash, then met Luke and another friend, Chad.

Ryan's plan was to roll and sell joints at an outdoor concert they had tickets to. Luke hadn't even known how much pot they had until Ryan showed him on the way into the concert and asked him to carry it because his jacket was bigger and bulkier. They'd already smoked a joint on the way, and Luke had been too young and too high to understand the potential consequences. Ryan's joint-selling venture fizzled, and after the show, they'd walked toward a burger place to get some food. A cop car had pulled up beside them, flashed his lights, and ordered them put their hands in the air.

Chad had run, but he and Ryan had been searched and arrested. Ryan's parents had hired a lawyer, and because he hadn't been carrying drugs on him, Ryan had ended up with probation. Luke's day in court had gone differently. It came back to him with painful clarity.

The courtroom was smaller than he'd envisioned, and it reeked of furniture polish. Beside him, his mother clutched her purse straps and pressed her lips together in a tight worry. Luke headed for an empty back row.

"Let's sit up front," his mother said, touching his arm. "It'll look better to the judge."

Luke didn't think it mattered, but he wasn't going to argue with her. Not here. They sat in the second row behind another young man and an older woman in a wide sunhat. It was obvious who the defendants were, and they were almost all men, many with brown skin.

The room was quiet except for the hum of the air conditioner. A young clerk sat up front on the dais, but the judge's bench was empty. How long would they have to wait? Luke just wanted it to be over with, so he would know what he faced. "What's going to happen?" he whispered to his mom. They'd discussed the possibilities to death already, but he wanted her assurance again.

"I'm sure it'll be probation and a fine," she whispered back. "It wasn't your pot, and you've never been in trouble before. Now hush until they call you."

After ten long minutes, the judge came in. The black robe intimidated Luke, but the man himself was a shrimp, five-seven at most and scrawny, with graying hair. The female clerk stood, so everyone else did too. Judge Bidwell called the session to order and told everyone to sit.

The clerk summoned the first defendant. "Jared Wilson, please step forward."

Were they going in reverse alphabetical order or randomly? Luke just wanted to get it over with quickly.

The man on the front bench stepped forward, and the clerk read the charges: public drunkenness and vandalism. The judge fined him fifteen hundred dollars and sentenced him to three months in jail, suspended, with probation. Jared Wilson thanked the judge, and he and the old woman walked out.

Luke breathed a sigh of relief. This guy was going easy on people.

"Luke Maddox," the clerk called.

He stood, legs shaking, and walked to stand in front. "Yes, Your Honor." His mother had coached him to say that.

"You're charged today with possession of ten ounces of marijuana and intent to distribute, both felonies." The judge's voice was bigger than his body.

The word *felony* made Luke's heart skip a beat. "It wasn't

my pot, Your Honor. I'm not a dealer." It was all he could say. Even though Ryan hadn't done the right thing and admitted he'd brought the pot, Luke wasn't going to rat on him.

"The report says it was in your possession. And don't speak unless I ask you a question." The judge was clearly irritated.

Luke wanted to explain, but was afraid the truth would make him sound like a thief as well as a pusher.

"I have no sympathy for drug users or dealers, because they all prey on innocent victims. Ten ounces is way more than enough for personal consumption, so I find it probable you planned to sell it. In addition, the young man arrested with you is only seventeen. So I find you guilty of the charge of corrupting a minor as well."

A pause.

"I hereby sentence you to ten years in prison. Bailiff, please take Mr. Maddox into custody."

It slammed him like a blow to the chest. He couldn't breathe, couldn't move, couldn't argue. The uniformed guard stepped toward him and grabbed his elbow. "But it wasn't mine," he called out, his voice weak, as the guard pulled his hands back to cuff him.

As he walked out of the courtroom, Luke glanced back at his mother. Her hand covered her mouth as she sobbed. It was the last time he saw her.

The wheels touched the tarmac and the plane bounced a little, jarring Luke back to the present. Abby woke up in the back and sputtered, "Where are we?"

"Southern Virginia. We're picking up Aaron."

"I knew that," she snapped. His girlfriend was still irritated with him for inviting Tara to join. The inner circle had formed all at once a year earlier when they were active in JRN. But the national group's failure to accomplish anything had motivated him and his friends to try more aggressive tactics. They'd only brought in one other person since, and Aaron had moved in with them and kept their secrets. But he was too sick to go out on most missions. The group needed someone like Tara, who had energy and ideas. And damn, she was sexy.

"What if Tara can't handle her assignments?" Abby said, going right back to arguing about his decision. "What if she freaks out when she learns what we have planned?" Abby had been complaining since they left Utah.

"We'll test her. Once Tara is dirty, she can't tell anyone." Luke regretted getting sexually involved with Abby, but she was passionate and smart and willing to risk everything for their cause. How could he not love her? He just wasn't in love. Whatever that meant.

The plane came to a stop near the hangar, where Aaron was waiting with a small carry-on bag. The analyst was thin everywhere, even his hair, and had a protruding brow. He looked older than forty, even without his glasses. "I told you he'd be waiting." Luke opened the door and climbed out of the plane to stretch his legs.

Aaron shuffled over. "Thanks for the lift. I hate flying commercial."

As they walked to the Cessna, Aaron said, "I've been analyzing data and looking at targets, and I know what we should hit next."

"I'm listening."

"Prison supply trucks. It's time to take the fight to the ground."

Chapter 3

Thursday, Oct. 2, 11:37 a.m., Washington DC

Dallas rolled out of bed, checked the time, and cursed. Last night, her second flight had been delayed, and she hadn't made it back until a couple of hours ago. Now she only had a few minutes to get downtown before Agent Drager texted her about their meetup. She pulled on yoga pants and a long-sleeve T-shirt, brushed her teeth, and headed out. She would grab coffee later.

The Acura she'd leased was parked in the basement of the rental complex in Georgetown near the university, so she trotted toward the stairs. At the last minute, she changed her mind and headed for the nearby bus stop. She hated driving in DC, and finding a place to park was a nightmare! Phoenix traffic was bad, but at least it moved, and the city's grid was easy to navigate. DC was a mess of diagonal streets, crowded roundabouts, and main arteries that stopped and started elsewhere. But the bus and metro system were both great, and the city was amazingly clean. Yet the air smelled a little dank, like the slow-moving river that cut through it.

Twenty minutes later, she climbed off at the intersection of M and 7th, and blinked in the bright warm sun. Fall was late again this year. Thirsty and irritated, she walked three blocks to a coffee shop, ordered a cup to go, and waited for

Drager's text.

Finally, it came: *Go into Midtown Cleaners, walk behind the counter, and enter the red door.*

Another few minutes, and she stood outside the dry cleaner business, one of many on the first floor of a red-brick building. Out of habit, she had glanced around while she walked, but no one had followed her. And why would they? She didn't know anyone in DC, except a few people from Justice Reform Now. The legitimate organization was national and had thousands of members, many of whom were here in the capital. The clandestine nature of their meeting was to be sure no one from either activist group ever saw her with Drager. She'd been involved with JRN since she'd moved to DC, so some locals knew her now.

Inside, the smell of hot chemicals assaulted her, and dozens of suits and dresses hung on a room-sized conveyor system. Did people really still dry-clean their clothes? A middle-aged woman behind the counter greeted her. Dallas nodded, rounded the counter, and walked toward the red door at the end of the short hall. *What was this place?*

Down a flight of concrete stairs, another door opened into a little cafe with booths along the sidewalls, and a short counter-service in the back. Only five customers, all men, three in dark suits and two older guys at a table in golf shirts. Did the bureau run this place?

Drager, in the last booth, waved her over. Under sagging skin, a thick nose, and weary eyes, his once-handsome face could still be seen.

"Hey, what is this place?" she asked, scooting into the booth. The previous time, they'd met in a backroom display of the National Art Gallery. They'd had little to discuss then, and she suspected the point of the meeting had been to build trust. She still didn't have much to report.

"It's a private café run by a retired agent." One corner of Drager's mouth turned up. "He worked undercover most of his career and likes the clandestine stuff too."

An old guy in a black T-shirt and white apron shuffled up to the table. "Hey, pretty lady, you're a sight for sore eyes."

"Thanks." The owner/cook smelled like burgers and fries, and her stomach growled. "Do you have a menu?"

"Nope. Just tell me what you want."

She hadn't eaten since lunch yesterday—if you didn't count airport cashews—so she ordered a grilled ham and cheese and a cup of coffee. Drager tapped his cup. "I'll have the same."

When the old guy left, Drager said, "I've got bad news."

Please don't cancel the assignment. "What's going on?"

"A retired judge named J.D. Bidwell is dead."

Dallas scrambled to place the name but couldn't. "Was he murdered?"

"Beaten to death with a tire iron." Drager raised his eyebrows. "MPD is handling the case, but I've asked to sit in on their task force meetings."

"How does his death connect to my assignment?"

"Bidwell is the Virginia judge who sentenced Luke Maddox to ten years in prison. So I think Maddox is a primary suspect."

That was worrisome. She'd known Luke was bitter, but he'd never mentioned going after the judge. "If it was a grudge killing, any of the ex-cons Bidwell sent to prison could have done it."

"Maybe." Drager gave a shrug. "But we know Maddox is aggressively seeking justice, and you overhead him say 'terminate.' That's why you're on this assignment."

In getting to know Luke, she'd forgotten that part of the overheard conversation. The fact that her target could be a killer sent a cool ripple of fear through her. But it didn't change anything. "It's good that I'm about to work my way in. The inner circle may have more hits planned, and we need to stop them."

"I hoped you'd see it that way."

Her thoughts came back to the murder. "When did Bidwell die? Maddox was in Utah with me yesterday."

"A parking attendant found his body this morning, and they think he died in the middle of the night.

Luke could have done it. "I made it back by three this morning, even with a delayed flight, so in a private plane, Maddox probably arrived before midnight."

"Or one of his activists could have carried out the murder, while Maddox went to Utah for an alibi." Drager's mouth tightened. "But a beating like that is personal, and I'd bet a month's pay Maddox is guilty."

But the murder seemed like it could be a setback to Luke's primary cause. Dallas kept the thought to herself.

Drager mistook her silence. "Maddox is dangerous, and you can back out if you want."

Would he have said that to a male operative? "I told you, I'm in."

"Good." Drager put a hand in his pocket, then slipped her a tiny device. "GPS. I want you to keep it with you. The inner circle seems pretty mobile, and I need to know where you are at all times."

As much as she wanted the security of that level of backup, it was risky. "What if they scan me before letting me into their base camp?"

"You think they're that sophisticated? Or paranoid?"

"Yes. Cree is a hacker, and I've heard them talk about someone named Aaron who's a tech whiz. I don't want to take the risk."

"It's your call."

"Besides, I bought a smartphone in Tara's name." The bureau hadn't approved the expense, but she couldn't stand the cheap phones for personal use. Dallas wrote down the number and slid it over to him. "I know you'll never call me on this one, but you can track my location." They would only talk on burner phones that had no names or personal information associated with them. It was the only way to protect her cover.

Drager's eyes contracted until he was squinting. "Have you thought about what you'll do if they ask you to help them commit an act of sabotage?"

Her jaw tightened. This came up often in undercover work, especially for agents who went deep into biker and drug gangs. She'd faced it before too, but snorting cocaine to keep her cover had been no real sacrifice. "It depends on what they have planned and how close we are to making an arrest."

"It's your choice, but you may have to defend it in court." Drager reached into his briefcase and handed her a small prescription bottle. "This is Rohypnol. If you get into a jam, you can use it to put someone else under. Or make yourself pass out, if you need to get left behind. But you didn't get it from me."

Relieved, she pocketed the bottle. "Thanks." Where was their food? She was starving.

Drager drained his coffee cup. "If you have intel and can't contact me directly, post a comment on the Real Food blog, and I'll start an online chat with you. I'll send a list of code words tonight."

"Okay. But I should be able to text or call on my case phone with specific details of their plans."

The old guy brought their sandwiches, set them down with a bottle of mustard, and walked away. Drager pushed his plate to the side and leaned forward. "We want to know the source of their funding too."

"Cree Songchild's family has money."

"That's an alias. The plane he flies is owned by the American Tradition Foundation, which is funded mostly by the Morrison family." Drager rubbed his eyes, as if they hurt. "And they aren't liberal. Whoever is bankrolling the inner circle knows what they're up to and may even be orchestrating it. I want to track the cash."

"You think Maddox is taking orders from someone?"

"Maybe. Get in there and find out. If we don't cut off the money, the donor will just find another foot soldier to do the dirty work."

"Consider it done."

Chapter 4

Thursday, Oct. 2, 3:55 p.m.
Back in the DC field office, Drager entered the conference room and found Agent Wunn seated on the right side of the electronic case board. *Damn.* Why did she have to be so early? He needed to sit in that spot to compensate for the blind spot in his left eye. No one in the bureau knew about the tumor causing the damage, and he didn't intend to let anyone find out. At least not until he could retire with full benefits.

"Good afternoon, sir." Wunn didn't believe in smiling. Still, she was competent, dedicated, and easy to get along with. Nice to look at too, but that wasn't why he wanted her on his team. It was just a bonus.

Drager raised his hand in greeting. "Hey. Would you mind moving? I prefer to sit there."

"No problem." Wunn gathered her things, including coffee, and scooted over.

"Thanks." Drager took a seat, wishing he'd brought his thermos of decaf. It still had caffeine, but nowhere near as much as the regular stuff, which gave him dehydration headaches and interfered with his sleep. But so did being an agent. He'd rest when he retired.

"I heard about Judge Bidwell's death," Wunn said. "Are

we going to be involved in the investigation?"

"It's a cooperative effort with me sitting on their task force. That's why—"

Rick Manning strode in, looking self-satisfied. Agent Two. The name popped into his head every time the little troublemaker and Agent Wunn were in the same room. Drager had sent Manning to the judge's crime scene as soon as he'd heard about the murder. He'd wanted to see it for himself, but he had to stay focused on their UC agent.

"I saw the body right before the medical examiner hauled it way," Manning said, still standing. "Brutal. I have a lot to report, but none of it is particularly helpful." He glanced back and forth between Drager and Wunn. "Do we know where Luke was last night or this morning?"

"Yesterday morning, he was in Utah, rock-swinging with our UC agent and most of the inner circle." Drager motioned for Manning to sit. This was his task force meeting. "Maddox was there until about two, along with Abby Gleeson and Cree Songchild. They flew back in a private plane, which stopped at a small airport outside of Emporia, Virginia around nine thirty last night, then landed at Centreville right after ten." Drager had spent the last hour tracking down Songchild's flight details.

"That leaves Maddox plenty of time to get to the parking garage," Wunn said.

Manning's smugness faded. "There are no prints on the tire iron and no security cameras in that area of the garage. MPD has its work cut out on this one."

Drager asked, "When are they doing the autopsy?"

"Tomorrow morning." Manning sipped his bottled water, then commented, "There are hundreds of defendants who had motive, and they all need to be checked out. MPD isn't

25

even focused on Maddox because he has no history of violence."

"Maybe our UC can get Maddox to talk about it," Wunn suggested.

"Not likely, but I'll ask her to try." Drager needed to update them on their progress. "Dallas has been invited to a meeting of the inner circle tomorrow around five. She knows it's a house south of Fairfax Station, and that's all."

"A breakthrough!" Manning would have high-fived him if he'd been sitting closer.

Drager grabbed the keyboard in the middle of the table and tapped the space bar. The case board with their notes lit up. "We'll soon know the names of everyone in the inner circle. Dallas thinks there's only one or two more she hasn't met." He keyed in the Virginia location and meeting time. It wasn't enough.

"Will she have a GPS?" Wunn asked, echoing his concern.

"I gave her a device, but she thinks they'll scan her and doesn't want to risk it." Drager had to let it be her call. "She has a smartphone though, so we should be able to track her."

"Once she's inside, we'll know what they're plotting." Manning rubbed his hands together in classic eagerness.

The door opened and Special Agent Garrick stepped in. "I just heard about Judge Bidwell's murder." Their boss didn't sit down. "Was Luke Maddox sentenced in his court in Virginia?"

"Yes, he's our primary suspect. MPD doesn't see it that way though."

"You have to nail him." Agent Garrick's downturned mouth twisted in frustration. "We can't let ex-cons take out judges. We need to send a very public message that we won't tolerate it."

"Our UC agent is about to join the inner circle and find out what they're plotting." So far, the inner circle had only flooded certain politicians with emails, taken down websites, and sent out phony emails to constituents. But he and Dallas both thought the group had serious sabotage planned.

Special Agent Garrick crossed his arms. "Don't be passive about this investigation or let it drag on. Let's get ahead of it."

"What do you mean, sir?"

"We need to lead the group where we want them to go. Let's set them up for a takedown that will send them to prison for a long time."

Whoa. Was he talking about entrapment? "I want to put them away too," Drager said. "But maybe we should see what they have planned. As long as we have advance warning from our UC, we can step in and arrest them in the act of whatever it is."

The boss shook his head and damn-near shouted, "I don't want them on hacking or vandalism or some petty bullshit! I want justice for Judge Bidwell. I want them incarcerated for life, so other activists think twice about joining their cause. Get creative and set them up for a big fall." The boss turned and strode out.

Chapter 5

Friday, Oct. 3, 10:00 a.m.
To kill time and blow off tension, Dallas spent the morning windsurfing on the river, enjoying the last of the bright summer days. After July in Phoenix, she'd been happy to move to Maryland for the fall, and the weather had been great. But she was restless now and hated the traffic.

She went home for lunch, then logged onto the Justice Reform Now website and checked their calendar. The national group had a demonstration planned in front of the White House next week. She wondered if the inner circle would be there. They were probably too high-profile now and not willing to risk even a minor arrest. A new blog had been posted on the site so she read it, stunned by the case it outlined. A mother of four in Florida had been sentenced to eight years for selling pot, a charge she claimed was trumped up. The JRN blog called for supporters to donate money to the mother's defense fund. Dallas hoped for the sake of her children that the organization was successful in getting the woman a new trial. Sending her to rehab made much more sense than putting four kids in foster care for nearly a decade.

Yet some parents, like her own, never got it together. Hers had snorted meth and drank themselves into stupidity during her entire childhood. She'd been passed from relative to relative, living out of an overnight bag, and her Aunt Lynn had paid for dozens of activities to keep her busy. Her parents had finally given up the meth, but not in time for her father's liver to recover. Mostly, Dallas chose not to think about them.

She clicked through to another blog. As part of her cover, she'd written a few opinion pieces and submitted them to the JRN website. They'd uploaded one, and she clicked on it just for fun. Writing was a decent pastime, but she could never make a real career of it. Sitting in front of a computer made her crazy after about two hours. She looked at the clock. It wasn't time yet. What kind of meeting would it be, and what did the activists have in mind?

Dallas got up and paced her little apartment, playing out possibilities in her mind. In the best-case scenario, the inner circle would ask her to join their cause and move into their house or complex. That level of trust and accessibility would allow her to gather intel quickly and wrap up the assignment. She was eager to complete this assignment. She hated living in DC. Once she'd seen all the historical points of interest, it was just a busy, touristy city. She'd kept sane by running along the river and learning how to windsurf. But she'd already been here for six weeks, and she missed Cameron. She'd flown to Flagstaff three weeks ago to see him, and it had been great—but also a little reckless. Once she was inside the group, she would have to break all contact with him. Her background profile for this case included a brother in Flagstaff, so she was covered for the trip she'd already made, but she couldn't go again. The inner circle might scrutinize her more closely for a while to make sure they could trust her.

Potentially, this was the most dangerous group she'd investigated. If they were willing to kill a judge just to stimulate public and Congressional dialogue on the subject of prison reform, they might well kill her if they discovered she was a federal agent. Dallas headed into the bedroom and pulled a small safe from under the bed. Inside, she kept two burner phones, one for contacting Agent Drager and one for contacting her friends and family. She let out a rueful laugh. That meant three people. Stacie, her best friend, had inspired her to choose Phoenix as her bureau location. Aunt Lynn, who lived in Flagstaff, where Dallas had grown up. Her mother was there too, but Dallas never contacted her. And Cameron, another old friend from high school, who was also her current lover.

She remembered that her therapist's number was in her phone too, but they typically conducted sessions through Skype. Dallas hadn't contacted Dr. Harper since she'd started seeing Cameron. Was she worried the shrink would disapprove? Or would Harper encourage her to get serious about Cameron? That might put an end to her undercover career. Dallas grabbed the phone and called Cameron, hoping it would go to voicemail, because that would be easier.

"Jamie. So good to hear from you." His deep voice dropped to a soft whisper. "Is everything all right?"

"I'm fine, but I'm probably going deep undercover soon, so you won't hear from me until the case is over."

"How long?

"My best guess is a month or so, but it could take up to a year." She knew of a UC agent who'd spent three years working a money-laundering case in Florida. He'd ended up divorced, of course.

"A year? Are you kidding me?"

"It's not likely."

A pause. "Promise me you'll be safe."

She almost laughed, but he was so serious. "Of course I will." *Liar!*

"I have an offer on the brewery. We're meeting tomorrow." He was trying to sell his business so he could move to Phoenix to be with her.

"Don't undercut your asking price on my account. I don't even know when I'll be back in town." Why would anyone who knew about her career get involved with her? None of her previous boyfriends had known she was a federal agent, assigned to undercover investigations. Instead, she'd called herself a government analyst. But Cameron was different, a lifelong friend who would be there for her even when their intimate relationship ended. So he knew the truth and would soon grow tired of her absences.

"You don't really want me to move to Phoenix, do you?"

True. And not true. "I do. Because I'd get to see you more often. But I hate to see you sell your business, your dream, when I can't promise any kind of real relationship."

A long pause this time. "You could give up undercover assignments. Maybe even ask for a transfer."

She knew he would ask eventually. "No. This is my specialty, and I'm not giving it up until I get the promotion I really want. Which would be an overseas assignment."

"You mean spying in a foreign country?"

"This is who I am. I told you upfront."

A sigh. "I know. But I can't walk away. I don't want to be with anyone else."

The thought of him with another woman gave her a jealous pang, something she hadn't experienced since high school, and with the same guy. "I'll do the best I can to be a good partner, but you won't think it's enough and eventually you'll move on."

"Do you hook up with your targets?"

The abruptness caught her off guard. "It's against the rules."

"That's not a direct answer."

"I sometimes seduce them. And engage in foreplay. But no real sex." *So far.*

"I'm sorry I asked."

"Think of it as an acting job. I'm getting paid to pretend to like someone and kiss them. It's no big deal. And not every case is like that."

"What about this one?"

Luke came into her mind. They had chemistry, and she knew he wanted her, but Abby was a mitigating factor. "Probably not."

"Good. Now tell me what you mean by deep undercover. It sounds dangerous."

"I'll become a member of the group. It's only dangerous if I break character or do something stupid, and neither of those things will happen."

"Please be careful."

"Always." *Liar!* "I have to go now."

"I love you."

"Love you too." She made it sound casual, like she would say to a brother. Which was stupid, because they'd declared their love for each other in high school. But she wasn't comfortable with intimacy. "Bye." Dallas hung up before it got weird. Usually, she broke up with the guy she was dating when she went on assignment. That kept everything simple and fresh when she got back. But she'd hooked up with Cameron when she'd flown home to see her dying father, and old feelings had surfaced for both of them. Sometimes she loved their relationship, and sometimes it felt like a burden. She'd have to discuss it in more depth with Dr. Harper—but not until after this assignment was over. Dallas laughed. She even kept her shrink at arm's length.

At three thirty she headed out, taking a small backpack with personal items, in case she ended up staying out overnight. At the last minute, she grabbed her lucky cloth and stuffed it into her jeans pocket. The keepsake had started out as a childhood blanket that went everywhere with her. As a young adult, she'd started cutting it in half and tossing large pieces. Now she was down to a two-inch square of fuzzy cloth that she liked to rub, and occasionally sniff, if she was feeling particularly insecure. Someday she would toss the last piece of it.

She walked six blocks to Saxby's Coffee shop on O Street and used her Tara Adams phone to text Luke and let him know where she was. Normally, she thought of targets and subjects by their last names—as everyone in the bureau did—but she interacted too closely with the inner circle for them to be last name only. Mistakenly calling Luke 'Maddox' when she was talking to another member could be a tip-off. But Drager referred to everyone by last name, which was fine with her. She hated the name Jamie and once she'd entered the bureau, she'd been happy to be called Dallas. Or Sonja. Or Tara. She loved slipping into a new persona and getting on a plane to go stay in a new setting. It was in her DNA now, after growing up in constant motion.

Luke texted back immediately: *I'll pick you up in 20 minutes. White van with blue lettering. Be outside and ready.*

The message sounded urgent and a little clandestine.

Energy surged through her body, so Dallas downed her coffee and walked around the block three times, barely noticing the DC architecture and multiculturalism that normally caught her attention. Seventeen minutes later, she stood in front of the coffee shop, waiting. She remembered Luke asking if she would break the law to further the cause. Would they test her loyalty? How serious would the crime be? The bright sun was warmer now, and sweat pooled at her bra line. When she'd infiltrated a prostitute ring in New Mexico, she'd snorted cocaine to blend in and had once delivered a satchel of cash to a white-collar criminal right before arresting him. But every nerve in her body was telling her this would be a whole new level of criminal participation.

Chapter 6

Five minutes later, a white van lettered with *Eric's Electric* pulled up, and the side door opened. She stepped toward it, and Cree scooted over to make room on the passenger bench. Dallas climbed in and pulled the door closed, the sound echoing like the slam of a jail door.

"Hey, Tara." Cree grinned beside her. "You wore black. Good instincts."

"I like to be prepared for anything."

From the driver's seat, Luke glanced over his shoulder. "Welcome." He turned back and gunned the van into the flow of traffic. Abby, in the front passenger seat, shifted to face her. "The location of the meeting has changed. It's happening right here, right now."

A hand clapped her shoulder from behind. "I'm Aaron." Dallas turned and nodded. Aaron said, "You came along at the right time. My body's giving out, and I just can't move like I used to."

Aaron was middle-age and gaunt, which made his brow protrude from his forehead. Did he have AIDS or some other wasting disease? Was he an ex-con too? Luke and Abby both had criminal records from long ago, but neither had been in trouble since their last release. She'd heard their personal stories—Luke's more tragic than Abby's—as well as perused their law enforcement files. But Aaron was new to her. "Are you all right?"

"I'm still here, so yes." He winked. "Thanks for asking."

She would sneak a peek at his ID later. When she had a last name, she would send it to Drager to research. First rule of undercover work: Know who everyone is and minimize the surprises.

Abby snapped her fingers, so Dallas turned back, suppressing her irritation. "What's the plan?"

"Sabotaging a fundraiser for Congressman Ralph Bletzo. He's the primary reason Texas has more for-profit prisoners than any other state. He's also blocking legislation to end mandatory sentencing. JRN has people protesting at every event he stages, but we need to cut off his money. We're working on a digital solution to empty his campaign account, but cutting off the flow is the best place to start."

Dallas' shoulders relaxed. The mission sounded relatively harmless. "What do you have in mind?"

"The main objective is to take over the A/V system and broadcast our message instead of his. Reporters will be there, and we hope to get the feed out live to a national news audience." Abby's eyes sparked with excitement. "It's a chance to tell millions of people about the capacity clauses in for-profit prisons."

Dallas had familiarized herself with their issues and understood that those contracts put pressure on states to keep private prisons full. "Can you explain the concept in a brief format? Won't we have to get in and out quickly?"

"We've already recorded our piece, complete with a slide show, and it's only ninety seconds long. Aaron will run the tech stuff from the van." Abby grinned. "You, me, and Cree will go in and lock all the access doors and shut down the AC.

We want the fat cats who put money into Bletzo's campaign to feel what it's like to be in prison, if only for a moment."

Dallas wondered what Luke would be doing but didn't ask. As the leader, he might simply be the wheelman, the one who got away to continue the cause if everything else went badly. But she didn't think it would. These people hadn't been caught yet, so they were obviously clever. Still, throwing her, a newbie, into a mission at the last minute, seemed reckless. "What building? Do you have a map? I feel unprepared."

"But you're in?" Abby challenged Dallas with her eyes.

"Sure. I can lock doors and move quickly."

"Sweet." Cree held out his hand for a fist bump.

Dallas obliged. At least he wasn't a hugger. "So where is this going down?"

"The Lincoln Ballroom at the Grand Roosevelt Hotel." Abby reached into her satchel for a set of blueprints and held them in her lap. A few minutes later, Luke pulled off into a small shopping mall area and parked under a shade tree on the perimeter.

"Scoot over," Aaron said, coming forward. He had a giant clipboard and set it in his lap. Abby spread out the building plans on the board.

Luke took charge and detailed the plan. "Cree goes straight to the central-air control unit in the basement. Tara goes up to the second floor to wait near the main doors. Abby will stand just inside the ballroom by the side exit. She'll text Aaron at the right moment to hack into the A/V, then walk out." Luke looked up from the blueprints and stared at Dallas. "When you hear our recording kick in, lock the doors from the outside, then take the stairs and get out." He handed her a shiny master key that looked fresh off the grinder. "Wipe the key and drop it in the first garbage can or drain you see. If you're spotted, run. If you're caught, refuse to answer questions. I'll be parked at the gas station on the next block over to the north."

Her pulse quickened at the thought of getting caught and blowing her cover. "What about cameras? They must have some security." Dallas let her nervousness show. It seemed natural for the situation.

Luke reached over and squeezed her hand. "Aaron will block the video feed when he cuts into the system, but the cameras are on these corners and easy to avoid." Luke pointed to four locations in the wide foyer outside the ballroom. "Keep your head down when you're locking the door, just in case."

Dallas visualized herself inside the building and memorized the camera locations by mentally nodding at each one. This was a familiar routine—with a different motive.

Abby handed her a hat with a wide, floppy brim. "Put your hair up and cover it. All that blond draws too much attention."

She'd worn it in a braid, but it was still noticeable. "I can cut my hair for future missions, if you think it's a problem."

Luke gave her an odd smile. "I like your commitment, but that shouldn't be necessary."

This mission wasn't any different from an FBI operation. Just less dangerous. But ending up in jail could cost her the assignment and send the inner circle further underground. So she needed more information. "How long will I be in there? How much time between when we set up and when we go for it?" She was careful to make her word choices sound like an amateur.

"Six minutes," Abby said, even though she'd asked Luke.

"Do I have a reason to be in the hotel? A ticket to the fundraiser or something? In case someone asks."

"You're just a guest, a tourist."

"Okay." Time to dig for intel. "Have you guys done anything like this before?"

Luke nodded. "We've run a few small missions, but nothing that's hit the national media. We're trying to start a dialogue and engage citizens to act."

"I hope it's effective. People tend to get worked up for a few minutes, then go right back to whatever they were doing."

"Social consciousness is dead," Cree declared.

"Let's wake it up!" Dallas said, feigning excitement.

"Damn straight." Luke started the engine and pulled back onto the street.

Near the front of the hotel, he double-parked for a moment, and Abby climbed out. Dallas reached for the door handle, but Cree stopped her. "Wait. We're not all getting out here. Too suspicious."

"Right." She leaned back and took a long slow breath.

"Nervous?" her seatmate asked.

"Of course."

Luke drove into the parking garage and headed down to the lower level. Cree moved to get out, squeezing her knee on the way. "See you on the flip side."

Luke circled back up three levels, stopped on the second floor, and turned to her. "See you in about twelve minutes."

"Unless I have a heart attack when I see the first security guard," Dallas said, keeping in character.

"You'll be great."

"Here I go." She climbed from the van and strode to the

elevator, glancing at the top of the concrete walls. Were there cameras? She tipped her head forward as she approached, just in case.

Once she was inside the hotel, she relaxed a little. Worst-case scenario, she would simply run and evade, a tactic she'd trained for. If she was caught, her one phone call would be to the FBI. They would get her out of jail, but her assignment would be blown. Or maybe not. The bureau was damn good at covering its tracks.

As she walked down the carpeted hall, moving casually like a hotel guest, Dallas scanned for cameras, tilting her head down when she saw one. The hat would do the rest. After two turns, she entered the main foyer, then leaned against the wall near the door as if waiting for someone and pulled out her cell phone. She keyed in a text to her neighbor at the apartment building, a college student she'd befriended to help establish a credible local residency, but didn't send it. The text mentioned she might be staying with friends for a while.

Well-dressed people, most over fifty, filled the lobby, some chatting in quiet tones, others walking toward the ballroom. She heard someone mention the cost of the dinner and another woman responded with something about "the cost of not re-electing him." Dallas recognized an older man as the politician they were targeting. He had a bodyguard behind him. Good thing they weren't going after him personally. The guard tapped Bletzo's shoulder, then pointed at his own watch. Dallas checked the time. Nine minutes to go.

Once the congressman entered the banquet space, the rest of the attendees quickly filed in. Dallas glanced inside. Fifty or so round tables, each with a floral centerpiece. The thousand-dollar-a-plate price tag for entry was a drop in the bucket compared to what Bletzo would likely raise in additional pledges tonight. If the sabotage was successful, nobody would have a chance to pull out their checkbooks, and the funds from the tickets might not even pay the expenses. A ping of compassion for the congressman came and went in a flash. He was a misogynist and a warmonger.

Dallas paced back and forth for a moment, acting like someone who'd been stood up. But her black jeans and silk tank top wouldn't make anyone believe she belonged inside the banquet. An usher in a blue uniform closed both sets of doors, and Dallas took a few steps closer so she could listen for the change in speakers. The usher pivoted and spotted her, then strode over.

Oh hell. Dallas looked down at her phone.

"Ma'am? This floor is not open to the public."

Ma'am? She was only 28. It had to be the hat. "I'm sorry. I didn't know. My niece is supposed to meet me here."

"You'll have to go somewhere else." His otherwise bland face puffed with authority. This was his moment to be in charge.

"My niece is only ten. I can't just leave." Dallas kept glancing at her phone to keep him from getting a good look at her face.

"You have to go now." He reached for her arm.

Dallas pulled away, not willing to get into an altercation. "Fine." She walked back the way she'd come, toward the parking garage exit. She planned to round the corner, then wait and watch the usher to see where he went. Completing her part of the sabotage felt important. She needed the group to trust her with their secrets. Plus, she liked to succeed. Giving up was not in her nature.

She went right at the junction and spotted two people coming up the hall. Business suits, maybe hotel employees. She glanced down at the phone, still in her hand, and slowed her pace. Talking rapidly, the men didn't stop or seem to notice her. Once they'd passed, she whirled around and trotted back to the corner. Alone for the first time since she'd learned of their plan, Dallas considered notifying her contact. But she didn't have her case phone, only her Tara Adams cell, and it was dangerous to connect it to the FBI. Besides, the bureau probably didn't want to bust the inner circle for vandalism. If the activists had actually committed murder or planned something equally criminal, the director would want her to stay undercover and gather intel for a bigger conviction. If she were in charge, that would be her call.

Dallas peeked around the corner and spotted the usher walking away from the double doors. She broke into a jog. She might only have a few seconds. Even if Aaron hadn't taken over the system and started broadcasting, she would lock the doors now anyway. It might be her only chance. The lobby was empty, and the usher still had his back to her. Mindful of the cameras, Dallas stopped and dug the key from her pocket.

As she locked the first set of double doors, a wild thought hit her. What if Luke and Abby had lied to her? What if they planned to set the place on fire, locking the rich donors inside? *Oh shit!* No, that was too heinous and would serve no purpose. She crossed to the second set of doors and hesitated. Trusting her instincts, she went for it. Hands shaking, she turned the locks and bolted down the hall. Dallas rounded the corner and headed for the exit to the garage. She would have to contact the bureau ASAP. If Aaron hadn't blocked the cameras, the FBI would use facial recognition software to ID all of them. Drager needed a heads-up. Heart pounding, she pushed through the exit and crossed to the cement stairwell in the parking garage.

"Hey! What's your hurry?" A male voice called from behind.

Security? Or maybe just a jackass trying to hit on her. Dallas broke into a run and pounded down the steps. Two minutes later, she was on the sidewalk and moving briskly around the block. Her first thought was to stop someone and borrow their phone to text Agent Drager. A trio of young women approached, and she paused. No. Luke or Aaron could be watching. Or Abby could be right behind her, after taking the same route. Dallas didn't have enough time to send a detailed text anyway, and if she were late getting back to the van, they might leave her. She needed to stay with them and learn their base location. The report would have to wait until she was alone or could meet Drager somewhere. Dallas kept moving and took the next side street.

When she climbed into the van, Luke asked, "You get it done?"

"Yes." She grabbed his arm. "Promise me Abby isn't setting the locked room on fire."

He pulled back, obviously disturbed. "Hell no. We're trying to change the system, not burn it down."

"Good." Dallas surprised herself and burst out laughing. "That was fun."

Chapter 7

After Abby scrambled into the van, Luke drove south toward Route 66. Behind them in the distance, sirens wailed, heading toward the hotel. Cree, who'd boarded a minute earlier, revealed that he'd almost been caught by a security guard.

"I nearly peed my pants!" He practically vibrated with energy.

Dallas felt a little giddy too. "An usher ran me off, but I circled back. The whole thing was surreal."

Abby laughed at both of them. "You think that was nerve-racking? Wait'll you hear what we've got planned next."

"What?" Dallas pulsed with eagerness to know.

"Not yet. We'll talk at the meeting."

Once they'd crossed into Virginia and the rush hour traffic had thinned, they stopped at a market. Abby made a quick trip inside to buy beer, tequila, and a couple of fresh pizzas to cook later. Dallas followed her in, but the store didn't have a public restroom where she could make a private call. They were back on the road six minutes later.

"Can I have a beer?" Dallas asked, her nerves still humming.

"Not in the car," Luke said. "We don't take chances of getting arrested for stupid little shit."

"That's cool." Her throat was dry and she wished she had

some water. "So, Abby, how did you get involved with JRN?"

Abby turned in her seat to face backward. "I saw a link to the website and started reading the blog. I loved what they were doing. After what I went through with the justice system—" She made air quotes around the word *justice*. "—I had to get involved. So I attended a rally at the capitol building, and that's where I met Luke."

Dallas had dossiers on all of them, but the paperwork never told the whole story. "Were you living in DC at the time?"

"I was at a recovery house in Arlington, Virginia. I'd only been out of rehab for three months and couldn't find a job." She patted Luke's arm. "But Luke got me hired as a dishwasher at the bar where he tended, so I was able to afford my own place and get more active in JRN. After we formed the inner circle, we all moved in together."

Dallas had been stuffing envelopes and making fundraising calls for the national organization too, as part of her cover. Repetitive deskwork wasn't in her comfort zone, and she'd hated every moment of it.

"What about you?" Abby asked. "Why did you join the movement?"

Dallas had rehearsed her lines. "Every time I heard about another innocent prisoner serving a long sentence or someone being killed in jail, I knew I had to do something. So I finally moved to DC to get involved. Justice reform is our most important social issue."

"Getting rid of drug laws is the critical first step though," Cree cut in, still too loud. "Without possession charges, we could close half our prisons."

Abby shook her head and launched into a speech about pushing for changes that voters would support, such as getting mandatory minimums. Cree disagreed, and Luke joined the discussion too. In the backseat, Aaron was sleeping. Dallas took it all in, admiring their passion for a worthy cause—but not their methods. The larger national group with thousands of members kept it legal, with petitions, protests, and boycotts. She respected that. But this small radical group had crossed a line—and who knew where they would stop.

Once they turned off the freeway and headed out into a rural area, Dallas paid attention to every turn, squinting in the near dark at road signs to memorize names. After another ten minutes, Abby handed her a folded bandana. "Put this on. Our base location is a secret."

Damn!

"I don't think it's necessary," Luke said. "She's in the circle now."

"We've never brought anyone to the base unmasked before," Abby argued. "Why should *Tara* be an exception?" Abby put just enough emphasis on her name to make a subtle accusation and gestured for Dallas to put on the bandana.

"I could get lost coming out of a paper bag, so you've got nothing to worry about anyway," Dallas joked as she tied the black cloth behind her head. Even blindfolded, she could still track the time and general directions, then let Drager know approximately where to find the place.

Fifteen minutes later, after a slow-moving left turn, she heard the crunch of gravel under their tires.

Cree touched her arm. "You can take it off now."

Dallas grabbed the knot and pulled the bandana off her head without untying it. Under a bright moon, she spotted big open spaces—agriculture fields, she guessed. At the end of the lane, a cluster of tall trees swayed in the wind, and beyond them sat a huge two-story farmhouse. Behind it were the outlines of several other buildings. The van stopped and Dallas opened the door, ready to stretch her legs.

"Wait," Cree blurted, grabbing her arm. "Let Abby go first. Her dog Treck is out there, and he's quiet but deadly."

Another good reason to keep from alienating Luke's girlfriend. After Abby and Luke both climbed out and greeted the dog, Luke pulled the door open. "Treck, this is Tara, a friend of ours. Be nice."

A pit bull, dark as the night, vibrated beside Abby's legs. Dallas decided to charm the damn thing just like any other member of the group. She grabbed the pizza boxes and stepped down from the van. Treck growled. She refused to be intimidated. "Hey, big guy. Get over yourself. I've got pizza."

The dog trotted over, sniffed at the food and wagged his tail. Relieved, she put out her hand and let him sniff her. If Treck liked pizza, he might be a beer drinker too. She would subdue him one way or another.

"He likes you." Abby sounded relieved and disappointed. "Let's go inside and heat up dinner. I'm starving."

They all moved toward the porch steps. At the top, Aaron turned to her. "Wait here while I get my scanner."

Thank god she'd left the GPS tracker at the apartment. She feigned ignorance. "What are you talking about?"

Luke stepped forward. "No. Let's go inside."

Aaron didn't move from the doorway. "I want to scan her before she comes in. It's my responsibility to keep us electronically safe." Aaron grinned. "You think the feds wouldn't send a pretty blonde to spy on us?" He nodded at Dallas. "No offense. I'm sure you're clean." Aaron went inside.

Well, fuck. But it wasn't the first time she'd been questioned by a member of a group she'd infiltrated.

Criminals tended to be paranoid—with good reason.

Luke caressed her shoulder. "Humor him and wait here, okay?"

"Sure, but I thought Aaron was just a techie. Is he in charge?" It seemed right for Tara's role to be a little defensive.

Abby and Cree pushed past her to go inside, and the dog did too.

Luke stayed by her. "Cree is the real coder. Aaron's an analyst who predicts patterns and can find information online. He's also a great tech guy, and we need him. But he doesn't run this operation."

Patterns of what? "He does sound useful."

The door came open again, and Aaron stepped out with a handheld frequency detector. It probably picked up signals from all kinds of digital transmitters, including bugs, trackers, and Wi-Fi. Aaron held it six inches from her body and followed her contours, making her feel a little naked.

"Let me see your cell phone." Aaron held out his hand.

Dallas pulled it from her backpack and looked at Luke. "Is this really necessary?"

He didn't respond.

"If the phone is the only electronic you have, we're about done here." Aaron handed the cell to Luke, and he walked inside with it. Aaron ran the scanner around her again. "Okay. We're good. Welcome."

"Thanks. I think." Dallas gave him a hundred-watt smile. "Let's go celebrate."

They ate at a massive dining table, with everyone laughing as they told favorite beer-and-pizza stories from high school or college. Dallas related a true account of vomiting pepperoni on a police officer after being arrested for public drunkenness, only it was her mother's incident, not hers. Abby announced she could top that story and detailed a blow-by-blow version of a time she'd sideswiped a cop car while high on oxy and mushrooms. Dallas glanced around. These people were criminals and targets, but at the moment, she enjoyed their company. Cree was funny and sweet; Luke was informed, passionate, and sexy; and Abby was entertaining. The activist's blogging skills translated to a verbal storytelling talent that kept Dallas' attention.

Around eight thirty, Luke said, "Let's move to the living room and talk strategy before we get too drunk."

Abby jerked her head toward him. "Is it too soon?"

"No."

Dallas knew they were talking about her and whether to trust her with their plans. She gave Luke a tiny wink for taking her side.

Luke stood and tapped Dallas' shoulder. "I'll give you a tour of the house while they clean up."

She started to protest that she needed to help with the chores, but Luke took her arm and steered her away. Cree threw a wadded napkin at her. "Don't worry, you'll be on kitchen duty for a week once you're not a guest."

They wanted her to move in? Excellent! It was happening sooner than she expected.

They walked under a wide arch opening into a long living area that was essentially two rooms, separated only by bookcases that jutted out on both sides. "This home was built a hundred years ago by the local doctor," Luke said, moving through the living space and into the square hallway. "These are mine and Abby's bedrooms, plus a main bathroom." He pointed at the doors as he talked.

He and Abby didn't share a room. Good to know.

"I'm thinking of trading rooms with Aaron," Luke said, his voice hushed. "He has pulmonary fibrosis, among other things, and may not live more than a few more months. The stairs are getting hard for him."

"I'm sorry to hear that. He seems young."

"He is younger than most who get it, but it can develop any time after forty."

"What are Aaron's plans?" Dallas asked, trying to be sensitive. "I mean, will he stay here? Or go spend his last days with his family?"

"We are his family now, but when it gets bad, he'll go stay with his mother."

"My father died recently." She hadn't planned to share it. In fact, she rarely thought about him, so it surprised her. Especially since his dying wasn't part of her background cover. She told herself it would be okay.

Luke put an arm around her. "I'm sorry. I know it never gets easier."

She liked the feel of him against her, but after giving her a squeeze, he stepped away. "There are more bedrooms upstairs, including an empty one you can use, but no need to look now. Let's get back."

The other roommates were in the main living room, Abby on one couch and the guys at an angle on the other. Luke took a seat next to his girlfriend, and Dallas pulled a cushion off the couch and sat on the floor. She wanted to see everyone's faces and not miss a single word.

Luke glanced at Aaron. "How are we coming on hacking into the political accounts?"

"Glad you asked. I had a breakthrough with Senator Pearlman's PAC, and the money should start moving soon."

Cyber theft? The inner circle was ballsier than she'd thought. "Why are you,"—she paused and corrected— "Why are we trying to steal from Pearlman?"

"He heads the Congressional Judiciary Committee and has blocked every effort to introduce legislation that would reform sentencing guidelines." Luke's response sounded practiced.

"But we're not siphoning his personal accounts," Abby explained. "Just his re-election fund. Without money, he can't run TV ads and could lose his seat, so he'll be off the committee. We have to get the old-school punishment people out of the way."

Dallas had heard most of it before in their post-adventure drinking sessions—but without the mention of their illegal tactics. "Are you focused mostly on drug laws?" she asked, keeping her eyes on Abby.

"Only as the cornerstone. We also want to get rid of all the three-strikes laws and mandatory minimums, essentially the same goals that JRN has." Abby shuddered. "There are people in prison for life because they stole a pair of gloves or some other petty bullshit."

After breaking the law twice before, Dallas thought but didn't say. Still, many repeat offenders were mentally ill and needed an alternative.

Abby wasn't done. "Sometimes I think we should kidnap someone like Senator Burton and hold him until something changes."

"Holy shit!" Cree spit out a mouthful of beer in surprise. Dallas was stunned too.

"Let's keep this real." Luke shot Abby a look, then turned back to Aaron. "When do you expect to breech the other two accounts?"

51

"I don't know. Maybe this weekend."

Dallas wanted to ask the names of the other financial targets, but Luke was still throwing questions at Aaron. "How much is in Pearlman's account?"

"Two hundred and twenty thousand."

"Nice. Once it's in the final offshore account, donate it to various political causes, with half going to JRN," Luke instructed.

They didn't plan to keep any of it? Weird. And admirable.

"What's next for us?" Cree asked.

"We've got the Virginia governor's push for more private-sector prisons and Ray Pearlman's vote on the decriminalization bill next Friday. But first, we need another round." Luke nudged Dallas with his foot. "Bring us all a beer, would you?"

Did he want her out of the room for the next discussion? Dallas got to her feet. "Do we have more tequila?"

"It's in the fridge too," Abby said. "I like it cold."

Inside the swinging kitchen door, Dallas paused and strained to hear what was being said in the other room. She heard Aaron say, "I'll monitor Tara's communications for a while until we're sure about her." *Damn!* That would make it nearly impossible to contact Drager. Then Abby started talking, and Dallas caught the words *plant* and *jail*, but Luke jumped in and discussion got fuzzy. Footsteps startled her and she stepped back. Aaron came through the kitchen door and stared at her. "What are you doing?"

"Getting everyone a beer." Dallas stepped back and yanked open the fridge. "Do you want one?"

He squinted, assessing her for a moment. "Sure."

She grabbed a bottle of tequila and a six-pack, wishing they'd bought a decent microbrew instead of this watery crap, but today she was Tara Adams, who didn't care.

Aaron followed her into the living room, pulling up a dining room chair, like someone who didn't plan to sit long. "When are we going to start disrupting prison supply trucks?" he asked, breaking into the conversation.

"I don't know." Luke's tone was leery. "We have to focus on legislation first."

"How are you going to get the votes?" Aaron was just as skeptical of Luke's strategy.

"Personal pressure." Luke grinned. "I think you'll like what we have planned."

After a round of shooters, Luke switched to a broader discussion about targeting politicians who supported for-profit prisons, but he didn't share specific details. Dallas excused herself and headed for the bathroom. She turned on the water for background noise, pressed a finger against the soft spot in her throat, and vomited up the last shot of tequila. As much as she liked drinking—and often used it as a tool to extract information—she didn't care for hangovers. It was also important to stay sharper than her targets. After vacillating about the risk, she added shorthand notes into her phone: *RPea/420 and pson sup T*. Hopefully, the notes wouldn't make any sense to someone searching her phone—if it came to that. They might not even make sense to her when she finally got back to her apartment and laptop to write a report. For each UC assignment, the department gave her a new computer with files and photos to support the background story they'd created. This time she had several Word files for books she'd supposedly ghostwritten and real photos of her in Flagstaff and Tucson.

Dallas hurried back to join the group. Rock music played, and Abby was dancing. The men were talking sports, so

Dallas joined Abby on the dance floor, loving the opportunity to cut loose. They partied for another hour with no more shoptalk, and Aaron was the first to call it a night. He excused himself and headed upstairs.

"Let's see if we made the evening news." Luke muted the music and turned on the TV.

They waited through the end of a program and a few minutes of world news about ISIS and Ebola before the newscaster brought the focus back to Virginia. The congressman's fundraiser came first, with the newscaster saying, "A group of activists hijacked the event and broadcast their own message of justice reform." The reporter also highlighted how the doors had been locked and called it "reckless," implying the police could press kidnapping charges.

"Is that true?" Cree asked.

"No." Luke shook his head. "It's just hype to juice up the audience."

Dallas wasn't as sure. Holding a person against their will was kidnapping. But she and Abby hadn't sealed the ballroom completely, leaving the access to the kitchen area open. She didn't comment though.

The newscaster played a segment of Aaron's recorded message and asked viewers to call if they recognized the voice.

"Oh hell." Luke clicked off the TV and looked at Abby. "Don't worry. The station will be flooded with names, but none of them will be Aaron's. And now people are thinking about justice reform."

The room was quiet, the party over.

Dallas stood and said, "I assume no one's taking me home tonight." She laughed. "Luke, you couldn't even walk straight on your last trip to the bathroom." Good thing she'd brought a backpack with a toothbrush and a fresh shirt.

"Hey, that was my full bladder making me off balance." He winked.

"Right." Dallas looked at Abby, deferring to her as the woman of the house. "Where do I sleep?"

"I'll show you." Abby got up, staggered, then collapsed back on the couch.

Dallas laughed again, feeling a little lightheaded herself. "Just tell me which room upstairs."

"The one in the middle," Luke said, helping Abby back up. He put an arm around his girlfriend and walked her toward the hall.

Dallas started up the stairs, and Cree followed. At her bedroom door, he grabbed her arm. "Tara, I have to tell you something." His speech was slurred, and a little spit drooled down his chin.

"What?"

"Be careful."

"What do you mean?"

"Remember when you told us at the rock swing that you had lock-picking skills?" It took him a few tries to finally get it all out.

A shiver of concern. "Yes. What about it?"

"They want you to use them, and it's risky."

"Doing what?"

"I can't tell you, but you'll know soon enough." Cree staggered to the room next door.

Dallas was intrigued, but too drunk to worry about it at the moment. She ducked into the bathroom on the second floor and brushed her teeth. When she came out, Luke was waiting in the hall. He grabbed her shoulders and pulled her in for a hot, salty kiss. Sparks shot through her, and Dallas kissed him back. Before she could decide how far she would go, he pulled away.

"Jus' wanted to kiss you goodnight." Luke grabbed the railing and headed back downstairs.

Chapter 8

Saturday, Oct. 4, 7:45 a.m.

Dallas woke, her mouth dry and sour, and her head filled with strange images from her dreams. Tequila did that to her. She threw back the quilt and stood, head pounding. Thank goodness she'd puked up that last shot. She dug aspirin out of her backpack and bolted for the bathroom in the hall. After a pee and a glass of water, she felt a little better.

The house was quiet, but outside a rooster crowed, and in the distance she heard machinery. Maybe a tractor. Back in her room, she looked around, seeing it fully for the first time. It was larger than she'd expected and had a small alcove that held a narrow desk. The two doors made her curious, so she peeked in both: a closet and a private half bath. Nice. She hated sharing a bathroom with guys. It had nothing to do with modesty or privacy. In college, after a few shots of tequila, she'd run naked through a crowded mall on a bet. She just couldn't stand piss on the floor.

Had they cleared out this bedroom for her? She remembered Cree's whispered warning on the stairs. He'd hinted that Luke had decided to recruit her after she mentioned her phony past as a burglar. That had worked well.

Dallas reached for her cell, wanting to text Drager, then

decided to wait until she had her burner phone. She pulled on yesterday's jeans and her clean shirt and headed downstairs. No one was up yet, so she made coffee and took her cup outside. Another glorious fall day with a blue sky and clean air. The leaves on the maple trees were starting to turn orange, and the fields they'd passed the night before were fallow. Dallas walked toward the back of the property, spotting an old RV, a horse barn, and a tool shed.

More important, she looked at the rising sun and tried to get her bearings, visualizing her location on the map. They were southwest of DC, about twenty-five miles she guessed, but with all back roads, it had been a forty-five minute drive. She didn't think it mattered. She was part of the inner circle now, and they talked as if they expected her to move in with them. That would likely happen today, so she would know the exact coordinates soon—and so would the bureau. She wanted to walk out to the main road and look at the address on the mailbox, but she worried that someone might be watching her. Instead, she took note of the vehicles. The white van they'd picked her up in, a black beat-up midsize truck, an old silver Corolla, and an ugly bronze sedan. She memorized the plate numbers of the van and Corolla, to jot down in her notes. She would process the other license plates later.

Back in the house, Luke was in the kitchen, pouring coffee. "You look great for someone who should be hung over."

Dallas chuckled. "I come from a long line of drinkers, so snapping back is in my DNA." Truthfully, her mother looked like shit after years of drinking and meth use. Roxy seemed to be off the hard drugs now that Dallas' father had died, but there was no reversing the damage.

"I think you're just naturally gorgeous."

"Thanks, but I'd rather not focus on it." She held out her cup for more coffee. "I think that's how I ended up in trouble after high school—trying to prove that I was more than just a pretty face."

Luke smiled. "You proved that at the fundraiser last night, and you'll have more opportunities soon."

"I'm nervous about what comes next," she said, playing her part. "I don't want to end up in jail myself."

"We all know it's a risk." Luke set down the coffee pot. "But we plan thoroughly. Plus, we'll set up demonstrations to happen during our next missions, so there will be distractions and we'll be fine."

Criminals always thought that, but shit happened. "I'm relieved." She shifted on her feet. "So what's the plan for me personally? Should I move some stuff out here and be on hand for the next mission?"

"I'm so glad you feel that way." Luke held out his arms.

Dallas set down her coffee and stepped in for a hug, watching the doorway for Abby. She had to walk a fine line between the two—seducing Luke enough to gain inside information while not pissing off his girlfriend. Dallas pulled back, not wanting him to kiss her again. Not in such an open place.

"Ready for breakfast?" she asked. "Or should we hit the road? I need to get back to my apartment, so I can shower and change."

During a long pause, Luke's eyes seemed to calculate several options. Finally, he said, "Let's grab some food to take with us. The sooner we get you settled in, the sooner we can move forward on a new project."

On the trip into DC, Dallas counted the driveways and houses between their location and the next main road. Almost as good as an address. But she suspected the bureau wouldn't raid this place until after they'd made a bust, preferring to catch the members in an act of sabotage. Luke surprised her by talking about Abby most of the way, detailing the blows Abby had taken in her life and how she'd become enslaved to the justice system, owing more money in fines and court fees than she could ever pay.

"If she missed a payment, she was in contempt of court, then they'd arrest her, and she'd lose another job and have no way to pay." Luke kept his eyes on the dense traffic while he talked. "So they would issue another arrest warrant and citation to appear. Each trip to court added to her debt. It's such a vicious cycle. A JRN donor finally freed her from it, and Abby dedicated her life to changing the system."

"I'm proud of her," Dallas said. "There must be a lot of people out there with the same story." It seemed like the right thing to say, but she didn't really know, because she'd never heard this side of the justice system before. Her father had gone to jail when she was young, but it had been about fighting. She didn't remember him talking about owing the court. When had minor crimes become a financial quicksand for people?

"There are a million people with similar stories," Luke countered, his voice loud with passion. "One woman spent three months in jail to pay off the fees she incurred after her minor son was arrested for possessing pot. It's insane!"

Dallas reminded herself not to sympathize with their cause, but those scenarios just seemed wrong—if they were true. "Take the next exit," she said. "My apartment is in Georgetown."

In the underground parking lot, Dallas said, "Thanks for the ride. I'll be back out this afternoon. I have a few things to take care of first."

Luke shut off the engine. "You can't bring your car out to the house just yet—for a lot of reasons. So I'll come in and help you pack." He opened his door.

Stunned, Dallas climbed from the van, scrambling to regroup. She hated the idea of being trapped out there. "I don't understand."

Luke walked around to her, his eyes guarded. "We have protocols, and new members aren't allowed their own transportation at first. We have to know we can count on you."

She scoffed. "You think I'm going to cut and run in the middle of the night?"

"Or worse." His expression was unreadable.

Dallas shook her head. "Whatever you're thinking, let it go. I'm committed."

"But for how long?" Still deadpan.

"Until we make progress." She needed to come up with something better than that. *What were their expectations, anyway?* She opted for humor. "Down the road a few years, if my biological clock starts ticking and I decide to settle down and have a kid, I'll come tell you I'm leaving." A dark thought popped into her head. "I do have that option, right?"

A soft smile. "Of course."

Should she press to bring her car or drop it? She suspected it would be a deal-breaker. "Let's go pack my stuff."

Luke stuck by her side as she gathered clothes and personal items. She had enough acting skills to pretend to be nonchalant, but his presence unnerved her. She'd never had a target in her home before. She was always prepared for it though. On every undercover assignment, she mailed a box of personal things to her temporary address, and this time, she'd sent extra clothes as well. But still, the place looked sparse even after living there for months.

Luke eventually commented on it. "You're the most clutter-free woman I've ever known."

"I've heard that before." Dallas zipped her over-packed suitcase. "There are advantages to non-materialism."

"I agree. Better mobility, for example."

"And no dusting." She grinned and set the suitcase on the floor. "Would you load this for me?" She needed him out of the space long enough to retrieve her other phones.

"What else are you bringing? We can take it all down together."

He didn't want to let her out of his sight! Had Aaron's mention of a federal spy triggered some paranoia? "Not much. Just my laptop and a small bag of stuff in the bathroom." Dallas stepped toward him, close enough to touch, but without making contact. "I can get the rest of my things when I come back for my car in a week or so, right?"

"Yes." He leaned in. "We're alone here, right next to this bed. We should make the most of it." Luke caressed her ear, a surprisingly sexy gesture.

"That's really tempting, but I'm not a home wrecker." Abby wasn't really her concern. She just wanted to get Luke out of her apartment ASAP. Her case phone was in a safe under the bed, and if it started ringing ... No, it was on silent, as always. Wasn't it?

"Abby and I aren't married." Luke pressed his lips against her cheek. "We're not even serious, just friends with benefits."

"She would be upset if we hooked up, and she would likely take it out on me."

Luke pressed his mouth into hers. The heat was overwhelming, and Dallas almost changed her mind. She hadn't had sex since she visited Cameron three weeks ago. And if not for Cameron, she would've indulged in a few stranger romps by now. Being faithful was new to her, and she didn't know how she felt about it yet.

Luke reached behind her to unhook her bra. Dallas broke off the kiss long enough to say, "Abby will know, and it could ruin things for the mission."

He stopped and groaned. "You're right. I have to break it off with her first. Then give her some time."

"It's the right thing to do." Dallas pulled away. "Why don't you put the refrigerator food into a sack to take with us, and I'll grab a few more things. Then we'll be out of here."

He grabbed her hands. "I like you even more now for respecting Abby. We'll be together soon."

"It'll be worth waiting for." If she could hold out. Dallas grabbed her laptop and stuffed it into her shoulder bag, fingers itching to send Drager an email. But she had to be careful. Aaron had said he would monitor her communication, but she didn't know how or what distance away was secure.

As soon as Luke was out of the room, she dropped to her knees and reached under the bed for her small safe.

"What are you doing?" He called from the doorway.

"Looking for my favorite shirt." Dallas sprang back up. "I thought I left it on the floor." Fuck the case phone. She probably wouldn't be able to use it anyway. Luke and Aaron were both a bit paranoid, and she would be lucky to send any communication at all from the farmhouse. She would ask to stop on the way back, then call Agent Drager on her Tara phone from a bathroom.

Luke gave a small smile. "I thought maybe you were getting out a gun. We don't allow them in the house."

"Good policy." She hated leaving her Kel-Tec too, but the assignment called for it.

A few minutes later, Dallas locked up the apartment, wondering when she'd see it again.

Chapter 9

Sunday, Oct. 5, 2:35 p.m.

Detective Jocelyn Larson thumbed through a stack of Judge Bidwell's court files, looking for violent offenders. The rest of her team was out in the field, interviewing witnesses and tracking down leads, so she was alone in the division, staring at paperwork and going a little stir-crazy. But someone had to stay in the department and take calls, in case another death was reported. She'd had too much alone time lately, and this wasn't helping. Working the late shift on weekends was always a challenge. It threw her whole body rhythm off, no matter how many times she'd cycled through it. Her desk phone rang, startling her.

"Homicide Unit, Detective Larson."

"This is Officer Romero. We have a dead woman at a construction site. It looks like she was shot and dumped."

Jocelyn's nerves jangled, and she was on her feet. "Give me the location." The officer recited an address off Central Avenue at the edge of the city boundary near Capitol Heights. "I'll be there shortly."

Jocelyn stuffed her laptop into her shoulder bag, grabbed a Mountain Dew from the mini-fridge at the end of the cubicles, and hurried out the back door of the District One building. Off to look at a dead person. Even after thirteen years, it still seemed odd. Outside, a blue-gray haze filled the sky, and the air was moist, as always. But she loved the fall when the temperature was perfect. In the parking lot, she passed rows of white patrol cars before reaching her dark sedan in the corner. The park-like area beyond the fence reminded her that the building used to be a grade school. The brick row-houses across the street reminded her that this was one of the capital's less affluent neighborhoods. Why the homicide unit for the whole city was stuck in this location was a mystery none of the detectives could solve.

She headed for the passenger's side of the car out of habit, then stopped midway. Her partner had called in sick, so she would have to drive for once. Typically, three or four members of a homicide team would go out to a crime scene, but this had been a busy weekend for murders, and for the moment, she was on her own.

The address was in a mostly residential area that still had a few patches of woods. Jocelyn pulled down the dead-end street at the edge of a neighborhood and groaned. A commercial construction site with a massive dumpster near the access. Law enforcement vehicles blocked the end, so she parked and climbed out. She passed two patrol cars, an unmarked sedan, an ambulance, and the forensic team's white van. Most of the responders were standing around, while the technicians gathered evidence. The techs were all civilians now, because the city council had recently decided they would be more objective than law enforcement employees and wouldn't try to manipulate the evidence—a problem she hadn't known existed. She was just glad someone else collected the blood, bullets, and bones. At the small-town PD where she'd worked early in her career, she'd had to do damn-near everything herself, including dumpster diving.

She spotted Officer Romero talking to a civilian in front of the nearby recreation center and decided to start there. She knew the officer from a department self-defense class they'd taken together. The woman was a no-nonsense perfectionist, which was probably why she liked her. "What have we got?" she asked, walking up. The center was closed and the parking lot empty. Too bad. It would have been nice to find a few witnesses.

"Detective Larson." Romero, thirty-something and stocky, excused the passerby and turned to her. "The victim was shot twice in the face, wrapped in plastic, then dumped in that gray bin." She pointed as she talked. "The project manager stopped by the site earlier to check something and noticed the smell."

Plastic might keep blood from dripping in the trunk of a car, but it didn't contain the stink of a decomposing body. "Did you talk to the project manager personally?"

"Yes. Mike Haywood. I took his statement."

"I assume he wasn't covered in blood?" She had to ask.

Romero gave her a tight smile. "Haywood was well dressed and seemed genuinely disturbed by his encounter with the corpse."

"Have the techs found anything?"

"Not that I know."

"Thanks." Jocelyn strode toward the metal construction bin, a ten-foot-long box with an open top. Wood scraps and chunks of sheetrock didn't decay and stink, so it didn't need to be covered the way garbage did. But if the project manager had smelled the body, it had been here a few days. Two coverall-wearing technicians worked inside the bin, and a third kneeled next to the corpse, which was now on the ground. The white plastic the victim had been wrapped in was still with her body, and the top half was smeared with blood. The technician had cut open the plastic to scrape the fingernails. The victim's face had been decimated by two bullets, and her blond hair was matted with blood. The black cocktail dress she'd been wearing at the time of her death was still intact. Jocelyn glanced at the victim's feet. No shoes.

She squatted next to the young male technician and introduced herself. "What can you tell me?"

"She's been through rigor mortis and is now soft and rotting, so she's probably been dead at least four days. But the ME will give you a more-accurate time of death." The tech bagged his scrapings, then reached into a carryall. He handed her a driver's license inside a zip-lock bag. "Sherry Jones, age thirty-one."

Jocelyn glanced at the license. In the photo, Jones wore heavy makeup and her white-blond hair had dark roots. She would run the name through the database as soon as she got back in her car.

"Where is her purse? And cell phone?"

He shook his head. "We haven't found them yet, but they may turn up in the dumpster."

Damn. Not having a cell phone was like investigating with one hand tied behind her back. "Any trace evidence on her clothes? Or signs of sexual assault?"

The technician picked up the woman's arm. "There's a bruise on her wrist, as if someone restrained her, but I haven't looked under her clothes."

"It's a classy dress." That bothered her. It didn't match the heavy makeup and over-blond dye job in the woman's ID. An upscale call girl? Jocelyn stood and called out to the techs working in the construction bin. "Find anything? Some black pumps? Or bullet casings?" The casings were wishful thinking. The woman had been shot somewhere else and dumped. But where were her shoes?

"Not yet."

A dead-end case if there ever was one. Jocelyn caught herself grinding her teeth and put in a piece of gum instead. She hurried back to the car, opened her department-issued laptop, and keyed the victim's name into the criminal database. Victims were rarely saints. Jones' record popped up, showing she'd been arrested for drugs and prostitution. So she was in the sex trade. Still a victim though. Two shots to the face seemed personal. A pimp, a john, or a boyfriend she'd pissed off. Jocelyn made notes of the woman's known associates and contact information. While the other members of her team were working to solve the high-profile murder of a retired judge, she would be chatting with prostitutes, pimps, and drug dealers. *The luck of the draw,* she told herself. Not everything was about skin color.

But it was right on course with the twists her life had taken lately. Her son, Kyle—the true love of her life—had left for college shortly before her twenty-five-year marriage had fallen apart. The sudden aloneness was challenging, but she'd finally found an activity to focus on a few nights a week, so she was feeling a little less lost. A rap on her car window startled her, and she looked up. Sergeant Murphy, her supervisor. Surprised to see him, Jocelyn climbed out to get on equal footing.

"Sergeant, thanks for stopping by." *Damn, he was tall.* She buttoned her jacket and straightened her spine.

"What have we got?"

"Sherry Jones, thirty-one, with a record of prostitution

and drugs. She was shot twice in the face and dumped here."

The corner of his eye twitched. "Give it your best shot but don't get invested."

Good advice, which she planned to take. Right up until she met the victim's mother. Then it would get personal. "How's Judge Bidwell's investigation going?"

"It's challenging. There are too damn many ex-cons to track down and establish timelines for." The sergeant gestured at the construction bin. "Do you need help with this one? Snyder said he had the flu and may not come in tomorrow either."

"Not yet. I'm heading out to locate her residence and hopefully a family member. They may know who did it, especially if domestic violence was involved."

"The team is meeting tomorrow at three."

They would be on second shift for a few more days. "I'll be there."

"Carry on." Murphy nodded and walked back to his car.

A medical examiner's van rolled down the street. Jocelyn waited for the assistant ME to climb out, then introduced herself. "Will you let me know when the autopsy is scheduled? I'd like to be there if I can."

"Sure, but it could be a few days. We're still processing the Franklin family murder-suicide, and we had a couple from a nursing home come in this morning. Likely suicide, but we don't know."

How sad. It reminded her to visit her mother soon. That had been the first blow in her string of negative changes—moving her mom to a nursing home. "Just let me know, or get me the report as soon as you can." But at least no one she loved had died. That had become the measure by which she evaluated everything. Jocelyn climbed back in her sedan, glanced at the address she'd noted, and headed across town to tell a family they had not been as fortunate.

Chapter 10

Sunday, Oct. 5, 2:40 p.m.

Luke cycled toward home, the afternoon air warm on his skin. After so much time locked up, being outside and free to ride was such a pleasure. Feeling pumped, he slowed and coasted down the gravel lane. They'd been lucky to land this place and rent it for the cost of the mortgage payment. The owner was the mother of a mentally ill man he'd befriended in prison. She had reached out to him after Charlie died, and they'd stayed in touch. When Hana heard he needed a place for an activist group to lay low, she'd offered the house because she was moving back to Japan—and because she'd lost her son to prison-guard brutality and wanted the inner circle to succeed.

Charlie's death lay heavy on his heart and made him think about another friend he'd lost recently. Robert, an ex-con who'd made a comeback and eventually run his own restaurant, was one of the only people Luke had loved after losing his mother. Robert had given Luke a job and a place to stay when he was at his lowest point and struggling just to survive. Being released from prison wasn't the same as being free. He'd had to report to a parole officer regularly for the first year and pay the monthly bill for his incarceration—while working for minimum wage. If not for the generosity of people like Charlie's mother and their anonymous donor, that debt would have hung over him for life, maybe even sent him back to prison if he'd failed to pay.

Luke climbed off his bike and tried to shake off the sudden blues. Feeling sad about the people he'd lost tended to derail his focus and drive. He'd long ago stopped feeling sorry for himself when he'd dedicated his life to changing the system that ruined so many lives—many of them decent people who just liked to get high. He parked his bike in the large toolshed and walked back to the house, his thoughts turning to Tara. Her energy and humor were just what the inner circle needed. Abby seemed a little burnt-out and edgy, and Cree was a rich kid who'd never been incarcerated and could go back to his old life at any moment. And Aaron only had a few more months to live. They needed someone solid, with fresh ideas and staying power.

He opened the door, saw Tara standing in the kitchen, and smiled. She was sweet to look at too. Classic beauty, with perfectly spaced pool-blue eyes, high defined cheekbones, and generous lips that begged to be kissed. He'd been mesmerized the first time he met her at the synchronized skydive and had been thrilled when she'd asked to join their after-adventure celebration. Cree and Abby had been charmed by her too, especially when Tara sympathized with their cause. Now she was here, in the inner circle, and Luke felt like all the shit that had happened to him had led to this point, to bring this incredible woman into his life.

"Hey, Tara. I hope you're cooking, because I'm hungry."

"You're in luck. Breakfast is the one meal I never screw up."

Luke kicked off his biking shoes and downed a glass of water. He could feel Tara watching him. They had to be careful to hide their sexual chemistry until Abby had adjusted—or left the group, which he almost expected her to do. That would be too bad. Luke grabbed a kitchen towel and playfully snapped it toward Tara. "I'll be back after I shower."

Abby walked into the kitchen. "Has anyone seen Treck? I think he's been missing since last night."

Luke realized the dog hadn't been underfoot in the kitchen as usual. "I haven't. I'm sure he'll turn up."

Abby gave him a blistering look as he passed her on the way out. Luke made up his mind. He would break off with her today. The inner circle's goals were too important to compromise with in-fighting. Their next few missions were riskier than anything they'd done so far, and they needed to be a cohesive team. After those outings, they would probably back off for a while. They might eventually move to another part of the country to start up again. There were politicians everywhere to target, but those with the worst views on justice were concentrated in the south.

Still, even from their current home base, they had conducted email campaigns with governors in several states, bombarding them with case histories of ruined lives and hacking into state websites to upload their own messages. They'd also uploaded and published lists of people who'd been declared innocent and released after years of incarceration. By scattering their efforts, they'd hoped to stay off the radar of the feds. But after the fundraiser sabotage they'd just conducted, the bureau was probably looking for them. The FBI had likely been monitoring JRN all along, and was now taking a closer look. Luke had stepped back from his role in the larger group years ago, frustrated by their lack of progress. He'd planned, recruited, and waited for a year after disappearing off their website, so he wouldn't be a suspect when the inner circle launched its direct assaults. The main goal was to ignite so much national discussion that voters would start to care about the issue, which meant politicians had to be responsive. JRN was making progress—such as finally getting marijuana reclassification to come up for a vote—but no one expected it to pass. And people quickly forgot news stories about legislation, because they had no faith in it anymore. It was time for another direct assault.

After breakfast, Luke took his laptop and some lined paper out to the porch. Being outside stimulated his thoughts and the words flowed better. But this post was easy, just a call to action in major cities across the country. Bringing out protestors was more than just a media-grabbing ploy. It also distracted police forces and kept the FBI focused on the people in the street. Meanwhile, they would hijack another fundraiser, then target Senator Pearlman later in the week. Luke wrapped up his blog quickly and uploaded it to their shared files. He messaged Aaron to have him route the blog through various proxy computers until it reached Jason DeSpain, the director of JRN. Luke never contacted Jason directly. They were friends, but he would never compromise the legal political movement by bringing law enforcement attention to Jason.

He reached for a piece of paper. The next letter was harder to write: *Dear Son. I hope you had a wonderful summer. I wish we could have gone camping together or just hung out at the public pool.*

Things he'd never done with his father.

I know you're back in school now, and I want you to study hard. Do the math, even if you hate it. Please say hello to your

Mom for me. I think about both of you every day. Someday, I hope you'll make the choice to see me and we'll make up for lost time. Love, Dad

He kissed the letter, folded it into an envelope, and addressed it, using a post office box for a return location. The kiss was for luck because he didn't know if Harlan received any of his letters. His mother might have moved again. She might not ever give them to the boy. He hadn't seen Molly since that day he'd walked into court and given up his life. Luke had learned he had a son after his release when he'd run into an old high school friend. Yet another loss. For himself and the boy. He would mail the letter the next time he went into town. They didn't send or receive any mail at this address, and he didn't put his name on paperwork anywhere. The utility bill was still in Hana's name, paid automatically from a holding account. Luke had considered an alias, but it would have made him feel like a criminal and a fugitive from justice. He wasn't either of those things. Never had been. He knew there was some risk in contacting the boy, but he and his mother were in another state now, and Molly probably tossed the letters as soon as she received them. As far as he knew, the feds weren't looking for him...yet.

Back in the house, he went to find Abby. She was in the dining room, hemming a skirt. The sewing machine had been in a closet when they moved in, and Abby had taught herself to use it out of boredom. She was a city girl at heart. He walked over and waited while she finished an edge.

She looked up. "Hey, Luke. Did you send the blog to rally protestors?"

"Yes. It should be up by this evening, and the first protest will happen Tuesday afternoon."

"I think we should take advantage of it."

"We will." He sat down, so he wasn't towering over her. "Can we go somewhere and talk privately?"

Abby blinked and her face tightened. "Should I be worried?"

"No, of course not."

"Then let's talk here. Everyone is in their own rooms. Except Tara. I think she's out wandering around."

Luke lowered his voice. "We should stop hooking up. We said from the beginning we didn't want to be a couple, and we can't let that dynamic hurt the group."

Abby's eyes blazed. "This is about Tara. You want to fuck her."

This would be challenging. He hated to lie, but he didn't want to hurt her either. "It's about keeping us all on the same footing and keeping the personal drama to a minimum."

"What drama?"

"I sense you're a little hostile to Tara, and it's because of me. So we should step back from each other. You and Tara need to be able to work together."

"You want her," Abby accused. "I think it's why you brought her in."

"We all brought her in. She has the right skills and commitment." Luke kept his voice low and calm. He needed Abby to be okay with this. "You know we needed another person, so I can hang back, then post bail or continue the work if everyone goes to jail." *Or was he just afraid of going back to prison*? Another stab of guilt. But keeping him out of the field had been Abby's idea and everyone had agreed.

She was silent, her eyes crushed, yet calculating. "If you hook up with Tara, I'll have to leave. I know we said we wouldn't get serious, but I'm not into sharing."

"I can't do this without you, Abby."

"Then make up your mind."

The back door banged opened, footsteps came up the hall, and Tara stepped into the dining room. "I'm sorry to interrupt, but I have some bad news."

Luke looked up, worried.

"Treck is dead. I saw him behind the old barn out there." Tara gave Abby a concerned glance. "He looked like he'd been sick. You know, like he ate something he shouldn't have."

Abby let out a cry and rushed toward the back door. Luke reluctantly followed, worried about how Abby would handle the dog's death on top of everything else. He wished he'd made the break from her weeks ago like he'd planned. Or had never started up with her. But a man could only be alone for so long.

Chapter 11

Sunday, Oct. 5, 9:35 p.m.

When the movie was over, Dallas glanced at Luke. The whole group had watched the comedy *Sex Tape*, and now she needed physical contact. Head-banging monkey-sex would be great too, but not likely. Luke had just broken up with Abby, and they needed to keep everything cool for a while. Luke headed for the door. Cree asked her to play chess, but she said she needed a rain check. Dallas stood and stretched, waiting to see what Abby would do. The other woman finally went to her room, still depressed about her dog's death. Luke had buried Treck for her, but Abby had glared at Dallas all evening, as if she'd had something to do with it. They were all a little paranoid.

Dallas heard Drager's voice in her head, nagging her to find out Luke's attitude toward the judge—as in whether he killed him—and to ask about their source of funding. She hadn't had an opportunity yet, but it was time. She stopped in the kitchen for a couple of beers and what was left of the tequila, then stepped outside.

"Hey, Tara." Luke called softly from the ratty couch on the wraparound porch.

"Can I join you?"

"Sure. But I'm in a strange headspace tonight."

She sat next to him on the couch and handed him a beer. "Strange how?" The evening was cooler now, but still pleasant, and the air smelled of ion and sweet clover.

"Mostly sad. I keep thinking about the people I've lost. And now I'm hurting Abby by breaking it off with her."

Dallas focused on his losses, which might get him to open up. "You mean a parent?" Her best guess.

"My mother. Yes, she was the first. Stabbed by a thug who wanted her purse." Luke turned so she could see his face. "You know where she was at the time? Outside the public defenders' office. She'd gone there to beg someone to appeal my conviction."

"Oh shit. I'm so sorry." Dallas handed him the bottle of tequila. "I suppose you have guilt about that."

"Of course." He took a long drink, wiped his mouth, and handed the bottle back. "I lost Robert too, an ex-con and dear friend who believed in me and gave me a new start."

"How old was he?"

"Fifty-seven. Lung cancer, the leading cause of death for black men over fifty-five."

"I'm sorry about him too." Dallas took a sip of tequila, feeling guilty about probing him for intel when he was clearly grieving. But it was her job. "Do you ever think about the judge who sentenced you?"

"Not really. I used to when I was still inside, and I checked up on him when I first got out, but not now."

Because he'd killed him and it was over? "Did you ever fantasize about getting revenge? I would have."

"Sometimes." Luke downed half his beer and stared out into the dark yard. "My biggest loss is my son. I've never even met him. But I hope to when he's older and he can choose to see me."

Unless she put Luke in prison for life. An unexpected stab of guilt. "How old is your boy?"

"Twelve. My girlfriend was pregnant when I got arrested, only I didn't know until much later."

She rubbed his shoulder. "Boy, you are in a funk tonight. What can we do about that?"

"A little more tequila and I'll just go in and pass out." He took another sip.

Dallas leaned her head against his shoulder. "Stay out here with me for a while. It's a lovely evening."

He kissed her forehead. "It's definitely getting better."

They sat quietly for a moment, and Dallas scrambled to find a segue into a financial discussion. "This is such a great place. How did you find it?"

"I know the owner. She's the mother of a man I shared a cell with. We have a connection now."

"You make those easily, don't you?" She touched his hair.

"Sometimes." Luke's voice was quiet. "Charlie was mentally ill, and I tried to protect him from the guards' abuse. That's why I ended up doing all ten years, long stretches in solitude, and no time off for good behavior."

"That's admirable." Dallas meant it. She respected people with the courage to stand up for the less fortunate. She sipped her beer. "What happened to Charlie?"

Luke put his face in his hands. "I can't talk about it."

"I'm glad his mother lets us all live here." *Was she the orchestrator of the inner circle?* "Does Charlie's mother know about the missions?"

"Not really. Hana knows our goals, but not how we achieve them."

Dallas lightly stroked his arm. "But she pays for everything?"

81

"Oh no. We have an anonymous donor who makes it possible for us to focus full-time on the mission."

"Oooh, a mystery donor. That's intriguing." She smiled at Luke.

"More like a mystery miracle." Luke suddenly pressed his mouth into hers, a deep probing kiss that made her want to climb on his lap. Dallas resisted the urge.

The front door banged open, and they pulled apart.

Abby yelled, "I thought you wanted to end the drama, put everyone on equal footing." She stomped over and locked eyes on Luke. "This is bullshit."

Dallas stood to go in, not wanting to cause Abby any more pain. "Good night."

She walked away, but Abby came after her. As Dallas stopped to open the door, Abby whispered from behind. "Stay away from Luke or you may end up like Treck."

Chapter 12

Sunday, Oct. 5, 5:45 p.m.

Jocelyn pulled into the small rundown complex and cursed at the lack of parking. Someone had taken the space in front of unit three, which had been listed on the victim's driver's license. She backed out onto the street and found a space a block away. Clouds had rolled in and cooled the air, so she buttoned her hip-length work jacket as she approached the apartment. Music and voices came through the door of unit three, and a couple argued in an apartment upstairs. The builder hadn't invested any money in sound cushioning. Who was in the victim's apartment? Family? A boyfriend? Or Sherry's pimp? The weight of the Glock at her side comforted her. Jocelyn knocked loudly.

A shuffling noise inside, as if things were being moved. Finally, the door opened halfway, and a big man in his late twenties looked her over. "Who are you?"

"Detective Larson, MPD. Who are you?"

"Darrell. Why?"

She'd come to expect evasiveness and just worked around it. "How do you know Sherry Jones?"

"I don't know who you' talking about."

Jocelyn reached in her pocket for the victim's license and showed it to him. "Does she live here?"

"No."

"Her license says she does."

"Must have been a while back."

"Do you know this woman?"

"No." His face gave nothing away.

Teeth clenched, she demanded, "Let me see your rental agreement."

"Why?"

"Because Sherry Jones is dead, and this is the only address I have for her. If you can prove she doesn't live here, I won't have to come back with a search warrant."

A younger woman pulled the door open wide and mouthed off. "We've been here six months, and there ain't no Sherry. Leave us alone!" The renter slammed the door.

Jocelyn ground her teeth, not caring about the damage. She resisted the urge to barge in, cuff the mouthy little twit, and arrest her for obstruction of justice—because she didn't have time for it. The reality was that the victim had moved, and she still had to find Jones' home and her people. Otherwise, this case would be a dead end. No cell phone, no neighbors to question, no boyfriend to suspect. How the hell was she supposed to investigate?

It started to sprinkle on the walk back to her car. Jocelyn cursed and picked up her pace, refusing to run, which made her boobs hurt. In the car, she reached for her vapor device and inhaled some caramel-flavored nicotine. Someday, she would give it up too, but for now, it beat the hell out of cigarettes. She stuffed the vape back in the glove box, checked the time, and pulled out into the street. So far, she couldn't reach the victim's contacts, the crime scene techs hadn't sent any new information, and trying to access phone or financial information on a Sunday night was pointless. So she would have a quick dinner at her favorite Chinese restaurant, then attend her Sunday night class as planned. After pulling a weekend shift, she felt entitled.

In a low-lit room that had once been a textile factory, Jocelyn turned her rod slowly with one hand, a propane torch in the other. The damn pendant she was making was lopsided, and the blue and orange colors were running together into an ugly brown. But she wasn't ready to label the glass-blowing workshop as another failed hobby. She could do this—she just had to give it time. First, she had signed up for bowling, but she'd been too inconsistent for her teammates. After that, she'd joined a choir because she loved to sing. But the leader's bitchiness had quickly sent her on her way. Jocelyn had no patience for short-tempered divas. But she loved working with the heat of the blowtorch and the pliability of the glass. Even better, she didn't have to impress anyone or get along with her peers. Which rather defeated the purpose. The point of the extracurricular activities was to get out of her now-empty house and spend time with other people besides cops and criminals. She thought about the guy sitting next to her. Toby. Too young, but he had talked to her earlier, and at this point in her life, that was exciting.

Her cell rang on the worktable, where she'd laid it so she wouldn't miss a call. A 703 area code, Northern, Virginia. The number the victim had listed as her emergency contact the last time she'd been booked into jail. Jocelyn shut off the torch, set down the rod, and walked toward the door. "Detective Larson, MPD." She pushed outside the metal building, wishing she had a cigarette. Her vapor device was in the car.

"Why'd you call me? Is this about Sherry?" The caller's

voice was southern and anxious.

"Is this Shonelle Jones?"

"Yes, why?"

"Sherry used your name and number as her emergency contact. Are you her mother?"

"Yes."

Jocelyn hated this part, but at least it wasn't up close and personal this time. "I'm afraid I have bad news."

Silence.

"Sherry was murdered several days ago. Do you know who might want her dead?" Jocelyn's strategy was to jump right into asking questions, so the woman wouldn't have time to break down until after the call.

"Oh sweet Jesus." Mrs. Jones let out a long moan. "I told her to quit whoring around, that she'd end up kilt."

"Did Sherry have a pimp?"

"How would I know? We haven't talked since Easter, and we sure didn't discuss the particulars of her job." Her voice quivered, but she held on.

"Do you know any of Sherry's friends? I need someone to identify her."

"Her cousin lives in DC too. Sherry's been stayin' with her."

"Give me her name, phone number, and address, please. And where she works."

"Kaylin Parshelle. Just a sec while I find the rest."

Mrs. Jones fumbled with her phone and rattled some paper before finally relaying the information. Jocelyn offered her condolences and hung up. A lead, finally. Too bad it was eight o'clock on Sunday night. At least she'd notified the next of kin. The rest could wait for the morning.

When the alarm woke her, she reached over to shake her husband, who never heard the buzzing until the third or fourth ring. But his side of the bed was empty—because she'd asked him to move out. What a strange, sad day that had been.

Jocelyn headed straight for the shower, starting with tepid water to shock her into full consciousness. Technically, it was her day off, after working the weekend. But with a tough murder case, waiting another twenty-four hours would only make it more challenging. And as far as she knew, her partner was still sick and not likely to be much help.

She dressed in dark comfortable slacks and a light-colored blouse, like always, then had oatmeal for breakfast, another lifetime habit. What made her morning routine different from most other women her age was the weapon strapped to her side. What made her different from most other officers was that she looked forward to the day she didn't have to wear it.

She stopped at the District One building on M Street to check in with Sergeant Murphy, check her voicemails, and see if her partner had made it to work. He hadn't. She tried not to envy his case of the flu. This investigation wasn't that bad. No one from the forensics department had called either. Jocelyn headed back out, hoping to catch Kaylin Parshelle at her workplace that morning.

The coffee shop was near the American University, a tedious drive north, and by the time she arrived, the early-morning rush was over. At the counter, a thirty-something woman picked up empty plates. She had light-brown skin and reddish-blond hair, an unusual combination.

"I need to talk to Kaylin Parshelle."

The waitress' eyes tightened with distrust. "That's me. What do you want? I'm working."

Jocelyn showed her badge. "Do you know Sherry Jones?"

The woman's tightened with worry. "She's my cousin, but I haven't seen her in a few days. Is she in trouble?"

A man at the counter got up to leave, and Parshelle thanked him.

"Can we go somewhere private?" Jocelyn asked.

"This is gonna be bad." The cousin let out a long sigh. "Just tell me."

"Sherry was murdered. Can you help me identify her?"

Parshelle blinked and pressed her lips together, fighting for control. "If I have to. Let me tell my boss."

"I'll drive you to the morgue, and we can talk on the way."

What little she'd learned gave her no help in pinpointing who'd killed Sherry. The victim's life had gone astray at twenty when she'd moved into the city and got involved with a thug, who'd pushed her into prostitution. According to her cousin, Sherry had cycled in and out of the lifestyle and jail, but no longer had a pimp.

They drove to the new Consolidated Forensic Laboratory, where the medical examiners had moved recently to share space with the evidence-processing technicians. Typically, family members made identifications through headshot photos only, but because the victim had been shot in the face, Jocelyn requested to view pictures of her body as well. The assistant at the ID desk clicked her keyboard, waited for the files to load, then turned the monitor toward them.

Four images lined up on the screen, the first one a close-up of the victim's face. "You can click on any photo to enlarge it," the assistant said, nonchalant.

Parshelle sucked in her breath.

Jocelyn had a pang of sympathy for the cousin. The headshots were gruesome, and no one wanted to look at a dead relative's naked body.

"I don't—" Parshelle stopped, grabbed the mouse, and enlarged a photo of the victim's torso. "That's not my cousin. This girl is too pale, and her boobs are different sizes. Sherry's flawless."

Chapter 13

Monday, Oct. 6, 8:30 a.m.

Dallas pulled her hair into a ponytail-knot and slipped on her athletic shoes. She couldn't wait to get out of the house. They were only going out to do some local rock climbing, but she was eager. Forty-eight hours at the remote farmhouse had made her stir-crazy. No opportunities for spying had emerged, and she'd learned no new details about their plans. Luke was keeping quiet about the next mission. She'd spent time writing and posting a political blog and editing a Word manuscript the bureau had provided as part of her ghostwriter cover. But it wasn't her thing.

She had also failed to contact Drager on the drive back Saturday. Luke hadn't wanted to stop, claiming that every time the van was spotted in the area it increased their risk. She didn't know how long they would monitor her communications, so she couldn't risk texting or emailing either. Dallas had never been so isolated from a contact agent on any undercover assignment. Even at the survivalist community she'd infiltrated, she'd been able to send email. She hoped for an opportunity today. Once they were out in the wilderness area, she might be able to wander away from the group for a minute and send a quick text. Or better yet, find a spot to make a call. Contacting Drager from her personal phone wasn't protocol, but without her burner phone, she had no choice. He would worry if she didn't check in and might raid the farmhouse too early, blowing their chance for a major takedown. If she had to, she could always reset the phone later to clear the data.

The group, minus Aaron, was standing around the living room when she walked in. Abby wouldn't look at her. Maybe she was ashamed of her bizarre threat the night before. Dallas hoped Abby would leave the inner circle, so Drager could pick her up and try to turn her against the others with the threat of prison. If Abby stayed, Dallas would do her best to charm her while keeping Luke interested, but at arm's length. A mission was happening soon, and she would get the intel to Drager come hell or high water. They could bust the group in the act, and this DC phase of her life would finally be over. Working her way into the group had taken months, and she was tired of living in the capital. Not that she missed Phoenix—the endless city in the desert—but she missed Cameron and Stacie and even a few co-workers in her own field office.

"Are you ready to go?" Luke asked. "We need to get moving. They're predicting rain for this afternoon."

"I'm set. I just need to grab some water on the way out."

Aaron came into the room, a pained expression on his face. "I'm going to the clinic. Anybody need anything while I'm in town?"

An opportunity to get away from the group! Dallas stepped over and touched Aaron's arm. "Why don't you let me drive you? You don't look well."

"Thanks, but you'll miss the climb." He gave a brave smile.

"I don't mind. It'll give us a chance to get to know each

other." Aaron hadn't participated in the earlier, out-of-state thrill adventures, so they'd never really talked. More important, she needed to contact Drager. Hopefully, she would also learn more about what Aaron did before she made the call.

"Uhhh..." The tech guy hesitated. Dallas sensed he wanted to say no.

"Oh, let her," Abby coaxed. "It won't hurt you to be alone with a woman."

Aaron blushed and joked, "I just don't want her to fall for me. Considering I can't make a long-term commitment."

Abby gave a polite laugh and looked relieved that Dallas wouldn't spend the day with her and Luke.

"Let's all get going." Luke turned toward the door.

Outside, Dallas followed Aaron to the ugly bronze sedan and climbed into the driver's seat. After exploring the property the day before, she'd documented the other two license plate numbers in her report and would send it at the first opportunity.

Aaron handed her the keys. "Thanks for this. Most days I'm fine, but every once in a while I can't get enough oxygen to function."

"Do you need a tank?"

"Maybe."

Dallas started the car, which smelled of sweaty blankets and rotting lunchmeat. She rolled down her window a few inches, noticing he wore a jacket and was always dressed warmer than everyone else. His disease was wasting his body, which probably made it hard to keep warm. She backed out, then headed down the long driveway. "Do you mind if I leave this open a bit?"

"It's fine." He buckled his seat belt. "Sorry about the

messy car."

"No problem." Dallas pulled onto the main road. She wanted to ask about his illness and his perspective on facing death, but she decided to wait until they'd talked about something else first.

"Did Luke tell you I was dying?" He seemed to have read her thoughts.

"Yes. I'm sorry. How long?"

"Four months or less. But I'm taking a new supplement that's helping, and I hope to be around to see some results from our efforts."

"I hope you are too." She admired his optimism but doubted politicians would ever make the kinds of changes JRN and the inner circle wanted. How many people really cared about prison reform? With 2.3 million incarcerated, it seemed likely that most Americans knew someone personally who'd gone to jail or prison, but for many families it was a relief when the addict or troublemaker was finally hauled off.

"What's your background?" she asked. "Why is this cause important to you?"

"My sister was murdered in prison, a place she should have never been. She was arrested at a bust of a drug house, charged with distribution, and sentenced to five years." His hands trembled in his lap. "Six months later, she was stabbed by another inmate."

"That's tragic. Did your family sue the prison or the state?"

"There's no point. Arlene is just another prison statistic. All because she got hooked on pain meds after a car accident." He shook his head. "I don't like to talk about it."

Dallas made the first turn, without asking for directions,

then asked, "Where's the clinic?"

He gave her an address in Arlington, on this side of the Potomac, and she only had a vague idea of how to get there. But they still had a long drive, and she had time to gather intel. "Luke said you were an analyst. What exactly do you do for the inner circle?"

"I use algorithms to search the internet and gather data. That helps pinpoint which targets to hit to be most effective in influencing outcomes. You know, like political analysts do."

"Is that what you did before you joined?"

"Sort of." He reached for the radio and turned it to a classic rock station, obviously done talking.

No problem. If she managed to contact Drager, the trip would be a success.

The medical facility turned out to be an alternative health practice that included an herbalist, acupuncturist, and homeopathic practitioner. While Aaron went in for a vitamin B shot and some other treatment she didn't understand, Dallas headed for the restroom next door at the convenience store. It would have better-insulated walls and fewer people to overhear her conversation. She purchased several bottles of Gatorade and a pack of spearmint gum, then asked to use the restroom. The woman handed her a key with a ten-inch serving spoon attached. Nice. So she couldn't put it in her pocket and walk out.

In a small space that reeked of both antiseptic and waste, she called Drager, urging him to pick up, even though the call wasn't coming from her case phone. She'd given him this number, so he should recognize it. On the sixth ring, he finally did, sounding surprised. "Hello?"

"It's Dallas. I'm on my personal phone. They monitor my

communications, so I can't report very often." She stood in the center of the bathroom, not wanting to touch anything.

"Where is their base location?"

"Wolf Run Road. Turn on the fifth gravel lane after Butts Corner."

"Good enough." A pause and Dallas sensed he was taking notes. Drager asked, "Was the inner circle responsible for the sabotage of Congressman Bletzo's fundraiser last Friday?"

"Yes, I was there. It was my initiation. Afterward, they invited me to stay at the farmhouse, but Luke came with me and watched while I packed, so I couldn't access my case phone."

"They sound a little paranoid."

"I think that will ease up in time." Depending on how long she had to stay with them. She wanted to wrap it up quickly.

"What else have you got?"

"I heard a mention of prison supply trucks." Dallas bounced on her toes, too hyper for the small space.

"What prison? When?"

"I think it's just an idea at this point, but they are planning to disrupt another fundraiser soon. Maybe even tomorrow. It may be last minute, but I'll get you the intel so the team can be there for the bust."

A pause. "My supervisor wants to take them down for a major crime that will put them away for life. I need you to push them in that direction."

Goosebumps rose on her arms. "What exactly do you mean?"

"Senator Ray Pearlman is blocking legislation they favor, and he's married to Stella Pearlman, the head of Safe America Alliance, the perfect target for them."

"I know exactly who he is." She'd become well informed

on the subject. "The inner circle has already been flooding his email box with calls for change and trying to cut off his funding."

"Great. Now all you have to do is to encourage them to target the senator or his wife directly, then relay the plans to us. I'll have a team in place to arrest them in the act."

Apprehension filled her gut. "What kind of direct targeting do you mean?"

"Something serious, like a home invasion with a hostage situation."

Holy shit! "I don't think they're a violent group. They don't seem to have any guns in the house, so I don't see them getting on board with that."

"You said they might hit a prison supply truck. They can't do that without weapons. They *are* that kind of group."

She remembered Abby's kidnapping suggestion the first night at the farmhouse and couldn't argue. "But it's entrapment if I suggest it."

"You're just going to speculate, put the idea out there. In the end, it's your word against theirs."

She'd never been in this position before and didn't like it. "I don't want to participate in a criminal act that could cause someone harm."

"You won't have to. Just push them in that direction, feed us the intel, then get out at the last minute. We'll take care of the rest."

"I'll see what I can do."

"This will look good in your file."

If not for her ambition to land an overseas assignment, maybe even transfer to the CIA, she wouldn't care. "I have to go soon, but I wanted to give you another name. Aaron Foster. He's an analyst and tech support. He's been with the inner circle for a few months, but he seems to stick to the farmhouse."

"I'll run him through the databases and get back to you."

A shot of alarm. "You can't contact me. They monitor my communications. I'm in a bathroom at a convenience store and lucky to have a moment alone. But I'll keep getting word to you, one way or another."

"Did you find out the source of their funding?"

She'd tried. "Luke claims it's an anonymous donor, and I don't get the sense that anyone but him is setting the agenda."

"What about the judge's murder? Did you get anything from Maddox on that?"

"I probed the subject, and he doesn't seem to have any hostility. But it could be that he's gotten his revenge and feels better now."

Someone knocked on the door. Dallas turned on the water and ignored her.

"Ask the other members about the Thursday night timing and what they did when they got back from Utah. See if anyone came into the city."

"Copy that."

"If things get hinky and you need an extraction, the code word is *liftoff*."

"Got it. I'll send a report when I can." Dallas hung up, deleted the record of the call, and hurried out.

Aaron fell asleep on the drive back, and the raspy sound of his breathing unnerved her. She kept looking over to ensure he was still okay. It felt odd to care about someone she hoped to send to prison. Picturing his frail body and gentle soul locked up with badasses tugged at her heart. Maybe Aaron would go stay with his mother before they were all arrested.

Dallas pulled up in front of the farmhouse, and Aaron shifted in his seat but didn't wake up. Good. She would use the opportunity to search his room. As she stepped from the car, he opened his eyes. *Damn.*

"Hey, are you feeling better?" She stood outside the car and braced against the cool wind.

"A little." He climbed out. "But I'm going to nap."

Just what she wanted. Dallas followed him in. She didn't have her own key yet, but they'd told her where to find the one they kept hidden outside. Aaron went to the kitchen, downed a glass of milk, and headed for his room. Dallas followed him upstairs, planning to kill some time on the internet while Aaron fell asleep.

For amusement, she searched for reports of the group's attack on Congressman Bletzo's fundraiser. The news media were no longer talking about the incident—except brief reports that the police had no leads—but political bloggers were. Which was what the inner circle had hoped for. It was strange to know she'd been involved in a criminal act that made the evening news.

Time to do her job. She tucked a flash drive into her pocket and grabbed her phone, in case she needed to take photos. It was risky to do on her personal Tara cell, but if she saw something significant, documenting it could be important. Dallas walked quietly down the steps and across the hall to Luke's room. The door was unlocked, no surprise, and after a glance over her shoulder, she hurried in. A quick look around indicated he was a minimalist and a bit compulsive. What little he owned was neatly organized. Not a dirty shirt anywhere.

A laptop lay open on the corner desk, and she sat down to

boot it up. A dialogue box opened, asking for a password. *Damn.* She'd expected it, yet it still frustrated her. After five unsuccessful attempts, she quit, not wanting the system to report the errors when Luke logged in next. She might as well get up and do a quick snoop for anything else. A dark rectangular box on the back corner of the desk caught her eye. A backup hard drive? Yes, and it connected to the laptop's exterior USB hub. Dallas pulled the flash drive from her pocket and plugged it into the hub. The drive came from the bureau and had been modified to automatically copy files when inserted. A beautiful thing.

Fast too. Three minutes later, she pocketed the little flash and continued searching Luke's drawers. Nothing interesting except a photo of a woman who looked like his mother. Why not keep it on display? She did a quick search of his closet, which held nothing but clothes, shoes, and outdoor adventure gear. No team sports equipment and no video game consoles anywhere either. Luke had spent his young life incarcerated, so he'd never accumulated the things young men normally did. He also kept his room as tidy as a prison cell. A little sad.

Dallas glanced at her phone. She'd been in the room for fifteen minutes. How much time did she have before Aaron woke up? She wanted to search Abby's computer too, if she could access it. Since Cree was a hacker, she wouldn't even try his. It might be coded to report any wrong passwords. Hell, he'd probably taken it with him to stay occupied on the drive.

Dallas crossed the hall to Abby's room, and the house creaked as the wind outside picked up. Was that rain splattering on the roof? Dallas reached for the knob and found it locked. *Curious.* Who didn't Abby trust? Or was the locked door a gesture to spite Luke? *Whatever.* Dallas went back to her room for her lock-picking tools, which she kept in a hidden compartment in her backpack. Both her purse and backpack were issued by the bureau's undercover unit, which had created all her background details and paperwork.

At Abby's door, she tried popping the latch with a credit card and it gave easily. This was an old house, and the locks had never been updated. Abby's room was more cluttered than Luke's, but she didn't keep many knickknacks either. Because of her troubled past? Or did the inner circle live sparingly so they could move quickly if they needed to? That would be her strategy.

Abby's computer was on her nightstand and already running, so Dallas was able to search her files. But all she found were blogs and poems Abby had written, a collection of photos, and some personal documents like an outdated resume. A glance through the browser history revealed an obsession with Pinterest, particularly jewelry and home furnishings. A look through Abby's closet revealed a sexy pirate-style costume and a collection of ankle boots. Weird, but not useful.

Dallas opened the top drawer of the dresser and rummaged through socks to find the bottom corners. In the back, she found a two-inch baggie filled with white powder. Abby was using? Was it meth, coke, or heroin? Not that it mattered. Dallas searched the rest of the drawers but didn't find any paraphernalia, like an addict would have.

She backtracked to the bed, lifted the top mattress, and discovered a handgun. *Well!* The weapon was a violation of the group's supposed no-guns policy. Balancing the mattress, Dallas leaned in for a better look. A small Luger with the serial number filed off. Why would Abby need an untraceable gun? She was obviously keeping it hidden from her fellow activists. Is that why she kept her door locked?

The sound of an engine rumbled in the yard below. *Shit!* They were back already. Her pulse quickened, but Dallas didn't panic. She dropped the mattress, smoothed out the blanket, and locked the door on her way out.

Chapter 14

Monday, Oct. 6, 8:16 p.m.
Luke sat down at his desk, turned on his laptop, and waited for it to boot up. The dialogue box opened, and a notice flashed: *Files downloaded.*

What files? Had someone accessed his computer? But how? He keyed in his password, a series of numbers that no one knew or would ever guess. Whoever it was hadn't gotten in that way. Maybe it was nothing. He'd recently downloaded photos of their rock-swinging adventure to a thumb drive, and maybe this was just a delayed message. Or had Aaron done a remote access/download? He would ask.

Luke checked his email, a web-based account that he changed regularly. The first was from their anonymous donor: *I can't fund your missions for a while. Maybe never again. I'm sorry. Best wishes. GJW*

The news crushed him. How could they continue? They had enough money to last another month or so, if they cut all the side trips and skimped on groceries. Cree always spending money, but it wasn't enough to pay Hana's mortgage, plus utilities, food, and gas. They would either have to move or get part-time jobs or find a new donor. Compelled to do something, Luke crafted a fundraising email, but didn't know who to send it to. They had to be careful about letting people know about their missions. For now, the inner circle had to accelerate its activities and get as much accomplished as they could before the money ran out.

To distract himself, he searched for political news and got another jolt. The governor of Virginia was giving a speech in Richmond the next day, and he was expected to announce that the state would turn over another group of its prisons to a private company. *Oh hell no!* It was immoral. Luke had been incarcerated in a for-profit facility, and now he knew why those prisons filled up faster than the state-run lockups. They had to stop this. He began to strategize, taking notes as the ideas came to him.

First, he would ask the JRN organization to flood the governor's email and phone lines with messages opposing the move. Then they would mobilize as many protestors as they could for the event tomorrow. A crowd of picketers would draw the media, and the public would learn what was happening. Luke wouldn't speak publicly, of course—the risk was too great. But the inner circle could hijack the A/V system and broadcast their own message, like they had last time. They would inform the state lawmakers at the luncheon of the real facts: For-profit systems had fulfillment expectations built into the contracts. Typically ninety-five percent. If the state failed to keep the prison that full, it suffered financial penalties, which negated the savings of the private system. The end result was that the judicial system, driven by economics, pushed people into prison who didn't belong there—people who otherwise would be put on probation, sent to rehab, or placed in a mental facility. It was wrong on so many levels.

Finished with his notes, Luke jumped up and rushed next door. "Abby!" He pounded on her door.

She peered out, her green eyes dull. "What's up?"

Had she been sleeping? "I need your help. We have to gather everyone we can to protest at Governor Slaybaugh's speech tomorrow."

"What's going on?"

"He's proposing to turn over more state prisons to CSA."

"Oh fuck. The asshole." Abby gestured for Luke to come in. "JRN has been pushing him to take back control of the one that's already private. What the hell happened?"

Luke stepped in, feeling strangely uncomfortable in her personal space. "The same thing that always happens. Someone offered him money to see things their way."

"What a setback." Abby shook her head. "Where is the speech? I'm not sure how many supporters we can round up on short notice."

"It's in Richmond, the capital, only a couple of hours drive."

"Your plan is to disrupt his speech like we did at the fundraiser?

"Yes."

"We have to stop him. It's time to step up our tactics."

Dread and rage fought for dominance. He'd never been a criminal and didn't want to become one. But too many lives had been wasted and too many more were at stake. If he and the others weren't willing to get radical, the cultural shift would be too slow, and a whole new generation of minority men could be lost. "Are you talking about framing the governor and giving him a taste of incarceration?"

"Yes. I've got the drugs." She reached toward a drawer.

What? "Why do you have them?"

"I wanted to be ready for this!" Abby's tone was sharp. She held out a small plastic bag filled with white powder.

Most likely meth. Luke repressed a shudder. "It's dangerous for you to even be around dope. Why take that risk?"

"I told you, I had an opportunity to acquire some, and I wanted us to be ready."

She was right that they had to get more aggressive. But he was glad he'd taken a step back from her emotionally. "Okay. We'll plant them in the governor's car, then report his license plate later for reckless driving or something. But with your record, you can't carry the drugs. You can't risk a long sentence."

"Tara should do it. She's the most expendable."

Reluctantly, he agreed. "I have some bad news. Our donor is cutting us off."

"What the fuck?" Abby put both hands on her head and started to pace. "Why?"

"They didn't say. But we have to act more quickly now. Once our money runs out, things could fall apart for us."

"What about the money Aaron hopes to siphon from the campaign funds? We can use that."

It was so tempting. "No. We're not keeping it. We're activists, not thieves."

Abby spun toward him. "Stop being such a moralist. Politicians are thieves! And law enforcement is sometimes more criminal than the people they arrest. We have to meet fire with fire."

Still torn, he wanted to postpone a decision. "Let's focus on this new mission first, then we'll all discuss funding as a group."

Abby started to argue, then stopped and shook her head. "Send me a link with details, and I'll contact the network."

"I'll do recon on the event building and get Cree going on

a hack of the sound system. We'll have Aaron record the voiceover." Aaron had volunteered to make the last one. If anyone captured part of their message on a cell phone, and the FBI analyzed it or tapped their phones, it could lead the bureau to them. Because Aaron didn't have a criminal record or much longer to live, he'd taken the risk. Luke hoped he would do so again.

He rushed back to his room, sat at his laptop, and crafted a message to JRN members, asking locals to protest at the governor's speech. He sent the text to his friend Jason, asking him to relay the message as soon as possible. The last-minute notice would limit the number of people they could rally, but any amount of distraction would be helpful. Now he had to conduct the security recon.

A quick search produced photos of the Lee Plaza building, but not enough information to plan a sabotage. He sent the links to Aaron, who could find anything online, including blueprints. Once they knew the layout, they could determine where the VIPs parked and how to access the area. The dual mission made him nervous, so he mapped it out.

Cree and Tara could handle planting the drugs. Tara would pick the locks and gain access to the back of the building and the private garage, then Cree would hack into the computer on the governor's car to digitally unlock it. That meant Aaron would have to take control of the A/V system. Aaron wasn't really a hacker, only a search-and-analyze specialist, but with Cree's guidance, the older man was picking it up quickly. They would have to get Aaron close enough to the system, then cause a distraction to send the security in the wrong direction while their message played. They could pull it off.

The question for Luke, as always, was whether he should

go in. The inner circle had agreed that he should hang back whenever possible, because he needed to continue the mission if everyone else was caught. But it never felt right. Yet, actively participating and risking incarceration again terrified him. Prison was so much worse than he'd ever imagined. The conditions varied from state to state, but in the south, they were often horrendous. He'd been beaten by the guards and sexually assaulted by other inmates. Almost everyone was. But solitary confinement had been the worst. Weeks, or sometimes months, with no human contact, very little food, and the stench of a leaking toilet that trickled sewer water down the concrete wall. He'd wanted to kill himself but hadn't had the means in his tiny hole of a cell. If he ever faced prison again, he would find a way to commit suicide. Ten, twenty, or thirty years would all be the same—a death sentence. If necessary, he would trigger a cop or a guard to shoot him.

The irony of it gripped him. A thousand people every year—who wanted to live—died while incarcerated. A heinous memory surfaced and he tried to suppress it. But Charlie, the mentally ill man who'd shared his cell for three years, haunted him. The oddball had annoyed the hell out of him at first. But he'd grown on him, and the more he'd witnessed the guards abuse Charlie, the more he'd tried to intervene. Until that fateful day.

The sound of his cellmate talking to himself had woken Luke early. Not that he ever really slept. The prison was quieter at night, but the noise never stopped. Toilets flushing, overweight men snoring, cellmates arguing. And the constant hum of generators. They also often left the lights on at night to punish the cellblock for that day's infractions. So true sleep was elusive. Just another form of the daily torture.

Charlie's demons got the better of him, and his chatter morphed into a loud argument. An inmate down the hall shouted for him to shut up. Charlie picked up a book and started pounding the wall.

"Hey, Char, talk to me," Luke said. "Tell me what's happening." Distracting him from the voice in his head sometimes worked to calm him down.

"The chip is signaling the enforcers again. He wants me to tear it out." Charlie didn't look at him. The man was thirty-six, or so he claimed, but he looked closer to fifty, with deep lines around his mouth. His eyes were gray and hazy and never quite focused directly on anyone.

"But you're here, where they can't get to you. Just ignore him." They'd had a similar conversation before. Charlie's morning dose of anti-psychotic medication usually arrived around ten. Hours away.

"The enforcers are everywhere!" Charlie started pounding again.

His cellmate's mental health had deteriorated rapidly in the last year after back-to-back stints in solitary. Luke had seen plenty of that in the years he'd been inside. People who were borderline depressed or bipolar often plunged into full psychosis after being locked up for a while.

The screaming started next, and Luke was unable to calm Charlie. A few minutes later, three guards arrived, equipped for an extraction. Normally, extractions were for inmates who refused to leave their cells at all, but Charlie only fought the trips to solitary.

"He just needs his meds," Luke said, risking punishment.

"Shut up and get out here," the guard yelled.

The metal door opened and Luke stepped out.

"On the floor!"

He dropped down, knowing there was nothing he could do. They just wanted him out of the way. The cellblock went quiet, as the prisoners tuned in to the extraction. Luke kept his face down, but looked up with his eyes. The guards moved into the cell, single file, the first one with a riot shield. The second guard carried a taser. Both shouted at Charlie to come out of the corner with his hands on his head. Instead, he mumbled profanities, begging to be left alone. The second guard stepped to the side and fired the taser. Charlie cried out and went down to his knees. The first guard booted him in the back, shoving him to the floor. When the poor man was face down—and still cursing the enforcers—they cuffed his arms behind his back, shackled his legs together, and looped a cord between the two restraints. Once he was hog-tied, they beat and kicked him until he was quiet.

Luke cringed at every blow, willing himself to stay still. He'd learned the hard way he couldn't help Charlie, only make things worse for himself.

Finally, two guards carried Charlie out, banging his head against the metal bars on the way. The third ordered Luke to return to his cell, then slammed the door.

A few inmates cheered as they took Charlie down the hall. Others expressed their disgust with the guards. Luke found some paper and with shaking hands, began a letter to the American Civil Liberties Union, asking them to intervene and get the mentally ill man transferred. The mail snipes would probably throw it away, but he had to try. His first attempt at activism.

Two days later, he heard Charlie had died in solitary, supposedly from a stroke.

Chapter 15

Tuesday, Oct. 7, 7:35 a.m.

Dallas tucked her phone and pepper spray into her yoga pants, pulled on sports shoes, and headed out for a run. She always carried the spray when she jogged alone, but it was worthless if someone really wanted to hurt her. On her last assignment, she'd run under a pier on the beach, and an unsub she'd chased earlier had clobbered her with a rock and dragged her into the water. Another reason—besides the Phoenix heat—that she preferred the elliptical machine, which was easier on her body. But she was stuck out here with no access to anything, and she really needed to burn off some energy.

The scenery was lovely, with groves of trees turning bright crimson and orange. An occasional car passed, but otherwise the morning was quiet. Between the trees, she caught glimpses of upscale homes set back from the road. The farmhouse where the inner circle lived was a relic of the past, the last one standing in what was now an upper-class rural suburb.

At the two-mile point she turned around. This was an opportunity to call Drager, but she had nothing new to report. The inner circle had a mission planned for the afternoon, but it was another event sabotage like the last one, and the bureau wasn't interested in the small-time stuff. Drager had made that clear. Dallas was still waiting for the opportunity to bring up Senator Pearlman and steer the group toward the takedown Drager had in mind. At dinner the night before, Luke had briefly discussed the next day's outing, then he'd gone to his room, and Abby had left in the van and not come home until midnight. Where had she gone? To buy drugs? Finding Abby's gun had made Dallas look at her in a new light, and she would have given anything for access to her car, so she could follow Abby if she left late again. Dallas thought about the GPS device back in her apartment. Too bad she hadn't been able to sneak it out past Luke.

No, she wouldn't risk calling Drager on her Tara phone again, unless it was something critical. Every contact she made had the potential to blow her cover and get her killed.

After a shower, she spent an hour online, reading articles on the JRN website and working on another political blog. She also visited the Real Food blog as a setup, in case she needed to use it later to contact Drager with critical information. She didn't think Aaron monitored her internet activities, but she had to assume that he might. Everything she did in this house had to build and protect her Tara Adams persona.

At ten, she went down to the kitchen, expecting to find her roommates preparing for the mission, but only Cree was at the dining room table, eating a sandwich.

"Hey, where is everyone?"

Cree shrugged. "Probably doing last-minute prep for this afternoon. It's an unfamiliar location, and the security could be tighter this time."

Jitters filled her stomach, and Dallas lost her appetite. It wasn't committing the crime that bothered her. Not something as low-level as sabotaging a political speech. Not after all the undercover work she'd done, preceded by her wild years in college. And she'd grown up with meth addicts, who'd broken the law on a regular basis. What worried her was getting arrested. She'd never been in jail, and she had some concerns about getting out. What if the inner circle didn't post her bail? The bureau probably couldn't help without blowing her cover. Dallas shook it off. The last sabotage had gone well.

"What's my role this time?" she asked Cree, standing across the table from him, too hyper to sit.

"I'll let Luke tell you. We'll be leaving soon."

"Should I wear running shoes?" Dallas mimed someone in a hurry, then laughed.

"Always." Despite Cree's smile, his tone was serious.

Dallas headed to her room to change. At the bottom of the stairs, she heard loud voices and paused. From Abby's bedroom, she heard Luke say, "Don't get started again. You'll put us all at risk."

Abby yelled back, "It's none of your business. You broke up with me, remember?"

"Don't make me kick you out." Luke's voice came toward her, and the doorknob clicked.

Dallas hurried up the stairs. What was that about? Started again with what? Drugs? In her room, Dallas changed into running shoes, pulled on a dark sweater, then stuffed a twenty-dollar bill into one pocket and her lucky cloth into the other. Not knowing what they had planned was both exhilarating and frustrating. She sensed they didn't fully trust her yet. After packing a few things into her small backpack, Dallas grabbed her laptop and stuffed it in too. She might have a chance to send her report.

Downstairs, Luke and Cree were in the dining room, and she heard Abby in the kitchen.

"Is Aaron coming with us?" Dallas looked at Luke. How should she play this? Still a little nervous?

"That's the plan." Luke turned to Cree. "See if he's ready, would you?"

After a few minutes of waiting, during which Abby made a trip to the van with water bottles, they all headed out. Luke fell back to lock up. As they crossed the gravel, Abby tapped Dallas' backpack.

"Is that your laptop?"

"Yeah, why?"

"Bad idea. If it gets confiscated, they'll track your communication to this place."

"I planned to leave it in the van."

"Why take the risk? Just leave it here." Abby stepped in front of her.

"Aaron takes his."

Abby rolled her eyes. "Aaron's computer is essential to his part of the mission, and he never gets out of the van. Just leave it. The ride into the city isn't that long."

Oh well. The report could wait. "No problem." Dallas went back into the house, trotted upstairs, and stashed her laptop between the mattresses where she kept it when she left her room. Someone doing a thorough search could find it, but at least she wasn't making it easy to take a quick peek while she was out.

They took the same seats as the time before, with Aaron in the back. Dallas turned to him. "Are you feeling better?" She hadn't seen him since driving him home from the clinic the day before.

"Fine as frog's hair."

She laughed at the expression. "I've never heard that. Is it regional?"

"It's from the past, and you're making me feel old."

"Sorry."

Luke pulled out onto the road. "We appreciate Aaron's experience and wish more middle-aged people would join JRN. Seniors too. Everyone knows someone in jail or who does drugs and could have gone to prison just as easily."

Dallas started to mention her father, then choked it back. Now that he was dead, it was harder to think about him. "I saw on the website that JRN is staging a protest in Richmond today. Is that where we're going?"

Luke spoke over his shoulder. "Yes, we plan to hijack the governor's speech with our own message, like last time."

"Only we have another surprise for him." Abby turned in her seat and grinned. "You know how I want to raise the stakes? We begin today with your burglary skills."

A wave of apprehension washed over Dallas. "What did you have in mind?"

"We need you to open a locked garage door, so Cree can break into the governor's car."

"And do what?"

Abby held up a packet of white powder. "This is meth, and you're going to plant it in his glove box."

That was why she had the drugs. *Devious!*

Abby handed the tiny plastic pouch to Dallas. "Maybe getting arrested for possession and having a felony conviction will convince the governor that something needs to change."

Dallas couldn't argue. Drager wanted her to steer the

group into something even more radical, so it would seem bizarre to protest this, then later suggest a home invasion. "How will you arrange for him to get stopped and searched?"

"Easy," Luke said, keeping his eyes on the road. "Governor Slaybaugh likes to drink at a downtown bar called Mac's. We'll call in a drunk driving report on his license plate, which he deserves, and the police will handle the rest."

"Where do you get all this information?"

"From the JRN network. The organization has people everywhere, and we tap into the database and connect with members who can help us."

Did those activists know what the inner circle was up to? Dallas tucked the packet of meth into her jeans pocket, wondering if she would have an opportunity to ditch it. "What does Slaybaugh drive and where will it be parked?"

"A 2009 charcoal-grey Bentley. We believe it will be in a private VIP garage connected to the convention center." Abby pulled out a map that looked like it had been printed from an online site, then pointed to a central location. "This is the building where the speech will be held, and the VIP parking is this locked area here. The van will be down the street at the mall."

Dallas didn't see how they would get away with it. "His vehicle probably has an alarm."

"Cree will be with you, and he'll jam the RF, disabling the car's locks and the alarm."

"What's my role?"

"To get into the back area of the building and pick the lock on the door to the VIP garage." Abby's voice challenged her. "You can do it, can't you?"

"Probably, but why I do I have to carry the drugs?"

Abby chuckled. "You're the newbie. That's how it goes."

Cree patted her leg. "Don't worry. We'll be in and out. Piece of cake."

Dallas wished she'd known the whole plan before she'd called Drager the day before. Getting arrested in Virginia for drugs could be devastating. What if she just said no? Again, she thought it would seem weird if she refused this somewhat minor thing, then suggested something more criminal later.

Luke spoke up. "Tara, don't forget there will be protestors, and we'll be messing with the sound system, so the security will be distracted." Luke looked back over his shoulder. "We wouldn't ask you to do this if we thought you'd get caught." He pulled onto Highway 95, heading south this time.

"I'm good with it." It was time to put Drager's plan in motion. "In fact, I'm surprised you guys don't have something bigger planned."

Abby, still turned in her seat to face the team, smiled at Dallas for the first time in days. "I like your thinking. Remember, I said that the other night too."

"That's what got me going on it." Dallas paused, not wanting to seem too eager. "Senator Ray Pearlman seems like the biggest obstacle to justice reform." She started to say more, then backed off. This had to seem like their idea.

"He definitely is," Abby said. "JRN members have been bombarding him with emails and case histories of devastated families, but nothing has moved him an inch toward reform."

"Have you looked for weaknesses?"

Abby's eyes widened. "You mean like something we could blackmail him with?"

"Or use as leverage."

Cree's leg vibrated beside her. "The pot decriminalization

legislation comes up for a vote Friday. If we could pressure Pearlman to support it, I think it might pass. That could change everything."

"Pass in the Senate, you mean." Dallas thought it seemed like a long shot, but JRN had been working on the issue for years.

"Yes, but that makes it a legitimate idea, and that's how the revolution starts." Cree was more animated than she'd seen him so far.

"Pearlman has a weakness," Luke said, suddenly. "A little terrier that he loves more than his wife."

Dallas tried not to laugh. "A dog-napping?"

"Why not?" Abby blurted. "If we take the dog, he'll vote the way we want and encourage his pals to vote with him. Then we give the pooch back. No harm done." She glanced at Dallas and mumbled, "Unlike what happened to Treck."

Everyone ignored the comment.

"I like the idea." Luke tapped the steering wheel. "It's time to be more aggressive. But we don't have to actually take the dog. We can just send a video from inside his house."

"What about his wife?" Abby asked. "Stella Pearlman is the chairwoman of that damn group that's opposing everything JRN does. We should threaten her instead. That way we get both of them to back down at the same time."

"No!" Luke snapped his head toward Abby. "We're not threatening a person, especially not in their own home. It's the same as kidnapping and carries a very long prison sentence."

Dallas felt relieved. She wanted Drager to get the big bust he was after for this investigation, but she kind of liked these people and their cause. Sending them all to prison for decades didn't seem right. Plus she was glad Luke wasn't a kidnapper. Then she remembered the dead judge. And the cyber theft. Stealing campaign funds was dirty business even if they didn't keep the money, so they had to be stopped. But no matter what happened, she wouldn't walk away from this one feeling good.

Cree asked, "So we would take the dog when no one was home?"

"Yes," Luke said. "Minimizing our risk."

Dallas had planted the seed and nudged them toward a major crime—now she needed details to report. "If the dog is inside and they have an alarm, how will we pull it off?"

Cree held out an electrical gadget a little larger than a cell phone. "This little baby will deactivate almost any alarm. It's how we're getting into the governor's car today."

"We should do the dognapping Friday morning." Abby was clearly excited. "The decriminalization vote is that afternoon."

"We'll look into it and find out what their schedule is," Luke said. "But it does seem like an ideal opportunity."

Dallas itched to relay the intel to Drager.

Two hours later, they parked at the edge of a mall in downtown Richmond. Blocks away, a crowd gathered outside the Convention Center. A few had signs, and some were seated, waiting.

Luke checked his cell phone. "The luncheon and speech start in twenty-five minutes. The protestors will begin chanting and enter the building about five minutes after he starts speaking. We need to all be in place before then." Like the previous time, he laid out a map of the area and blueprints of building, then walked them through the plan.

"Why are we going in a locked door at the side instead of

using the front like the guests?" Dallas asked.

"Because this is a private event, and we need to access the back part of the building." Luke gave her a quick smile. "You can do this, right?"

Dallas nodded. She was good with picks but not a pro. It all depended on the complexity of the system.

From the back seat, Aaron called out, "Get going. I need to focus."

"Let me find their system before I take off. I'm faster than you are." Cree reached over the seat and took Aaron's laptop. Two minutes later, he announced, "I'm in," and handed it back. "Let's go, Tara. We have to get inside and find the door to the VIP parking."

Dallas climbed out of the van, ready to stretch her legs. Patches of blue sky broke out between the clouds, and the Richmond downtown seemed clean and quaint. She spotted a police officer on the perimeter of the protest crowd, and the adrenaline started to flow. Cree hopped out behind her, zipped his jacket, and moved toward the street. Dallas hurried to get in step with him.

"Should we split up before we get there?" She wanted to get the meth out of her pocket. But if she did, would she be able to fake planting it in the glove box? Or would Cree be standing right there watching?

"Just walk ahead of me, until we get into the alley," he urged.

She picked up her pace, glancing at the businesses and scanning for places to duck into later, if necessary. She crossed Marshall Street, noticed the growing crowd of protestors, and turned left. A half block later, she ducked into an alley, as they'd planned. They didn't want to be seen together. Green trash bins dotted the narrow pass-through, begging her to ditch the meth. But Cree was right behind her, and there was no way to be subtle about dumping the drugs. It was probably too soon anyway. Cree might ask to see the packet at some point. She told herself it would be okay. The bureau would get her out of anything messy.

An employee leaned against the back door of a restaurant, smoking. Dallas nodded, pulled out her phone, and looked down at it as she passed. At the end, the alley intersected with another walkway that ran alongside the Convention Center property. Dallas went left again and crossed to the other side. She glanced around, didn't see anyone, then quickly scaled the six-foot cinderblock wall. Dropping down on the other side, she landed on a soft strip of grass at the edge of a courtyard. The few outdoor tables were empty, and she dashed across the flagstone to the door leading into the building. She glanced up. No security camera, which wasn't surprising. The meeting hall likely didn't keep cash or valuables and wasn't attractive to thieves. Bending over, she examined the lock. A combination keypad and standard keyhole. Most employees—if they ever came out here—probably keyed in a code, but the standard bolt lock ensured entry into the building if the power went out.

The tall concrete barrier around the courtyard gave her privacy, but as she pulled out her B&E tools, her pulse escalated. The meth in her pocket would get her more time in jail than breaking in. Fortunately, Tara Adams didn't really exist.

Cree dropped over the wall with a light thud. Dallas glanced back at him, then started on the lock, choosing a tool with a sharp double bend. She visualized the internal mechanism, then worked the pick in a side-to-side motion, hoping to catch both prongs.

"How's it going?" Cree was suddenly beside her, light on his feet for a man.

"I don't know yet.

He stood right behind her, looking over her shoulder. "You have to hurry."

"Give me a minute. Sometimes this is about patience and luck."

She was rusty, and it took longer than she expected. In the afternoon sun, her sweater was too warm, and sweat broke out on her forehead. But the bolt finally retracted. She held open the door for Cree. "Lead the way."

"You rock." Another fist bump as he walked past and stepped inside.

The door opened into a small foyer with hallways leading in two directions. The sound of a heat pump came from a nearby room, but otherwise the back of the building was quiet. The muffled sound of a roomful of voices drifted down the hall to the right.

Cree stopped and checked the time on his cell phone. "The speech has started, and Aaron should be cutting into it any minute. Let's move slowly until we hear the protestors trying to push through the front door. The police will try to stop them, and it will get loud. That will be our best opportunity." He turned to the left. "This way."

Dallas followed, worried about the meth in her pocket and whether she would have to leave it in an innocent man's car just to keep her cover. She would inform Drager, and hopefully the bureau could take care of it. After another turn, they spotted a steel door. A security guard stood near it.

She froze and so did Cree. They both took a step back behind the blind corner. Once they were out of sight, they turned to hide their faces, but didn't retreat.

Cree checked his cell phone again and held up two fingers.

Two minutes? Dallas' nerves were humming. She hadn't expected a security guard. Now she just wanted to get the hell out.

Muffled shouting came from the front of the building. Officers yelled, "Get back!" and chanters shouted, "No prison for profit!" Nearby, footsteps pounded away from them.

Dallas peeked around the corner. The security guard had bolted toward the action.

She hurried to the metal door with Cree right on her heels. After examining the lock, she pulled out her picks and selected one with a zigzag head that she'd never used before. Dallas slipped it into the opening, pressed left, and jiggled it.

An alarm blared.

"Oh fuck!" Dallas spun around.

Cree was already running back the way they'd come, his pack bouncing. Dallas sprinted after him, heart pounding. Maybe with all the commotion of the hijacked sound system and protestors storming the entrance, no one would check the doors. Maybe they would think the alarm had been set purposefully as a distraction. She rounded the corner and spotted the courtyard door showing beyond the outline of Cree's back. They just needed to get outside and over the wall.

The same security guard came barreling toward them. "Stop!"

Ahead of her, Cree grabbed the door handle, yanked it open, and sprinted through without looking back. The door started to close. Dallas lunged for it and missed. It slammed shut, and the guard grabbed her by the shoulder.

Chapter 16

Tuesday, Oct. 7, 8:45 a.m.

Drager scooted through security and hurried to his workstation in the DC field office on 4th Street. A few blocks away, fellow agents worked at the bureau's headquarters, handling national crises. As much as he'd always wanted to be part of the Critical Incident Operations Unit, he'd never put in the extra hours required to advance. Instead, he'd spent evenings and weekends with his son, and he had no regrets. But now Kyle was in college, his marriage seemed to be over, and he was free to dedicate as much time to his job as he was willing. Only now, he was tired and didn't care if he got promoted. He loved his work, that wouldn't change, but some cases were less interesting than others. This one, Freeman, had started slow, with the UC needing months to work her way in, but now it was rapidly picking up steam and could become a major takedown for him.

At his desk, he checked his email and voicemail. A message from Sergeant Murphy at the MPD homicide unit: "The Bidwell task force is meeting in an hour. I'll send you a brief if you can't make it."

Yeah, right. He would be there, and Murphy knew it. His desk phone rang, an internal call from the reception clerk. "Drager here."

"I have Senator Pearlman on the line. He wants to report a cyber theft."

What the heck? He needed to talk to Pearlman anyway.

Before he could respond, the clerk continued, "I know it's not your department, but he suspects an activist group, so I thought you'd want to know."

"Put him through."

"Agent Drager? This is Senator Ray Pearlman. I just learned that two hundred grand and change has been hijacked from my campaign account!"

"How?" Bank security was tighter than a duck's ass.

"Someone impersonating a bank employee called my campaign manager, who then sent an email with passcode information to my assistant. The idiot." Pearlman's disgust was evident. "The scammers must have intercepted the email, because the money was transferred to a Swiss account this morning. My bank is investigating, but I want the FBI on this too." The senator went back to being outraged. "I think it's the same group that sabotaged Congressman Bletzo's fundraiser last week. The pricks have also bombarded my email account and messed with my website. They have to be stopped!"

"We're working on it. Send me an itinerary of your events, so we can get field officers out there."

"I will. But what progress have you made? What about the hotel's security cameras at the fundraiser? Did they catch anything?"

The congressman had called with the same questions earlier in the week, and Drager had placated him too. "The group has a talented hacker who took control of the cameras as well as the audio system, so we don't have much to go on."

"But who are they? You must have some idea."

Drager couldn't give him names, because Pearlman would push for an arrest. He needed to ease the senator into the idea of a sting with him, and possibly his wife, as bait. "We think they're a splinter group of Justice Reform Now, and we may have identified the leader. So rest assured, we're watching him, but we need solid evidence before we move."

A loud sigh. "I understand. But can you get my money back? I'm in a tight re-election race."

"You'll need to talk to the cyber experts, but they're good." Drager decided it was time to get the senator involved. "Since the group is already targeting you, we'd like to get you on board an operation to take them down."

A slight hesitation. "Whatever you need."

Drager couldn't mention his UC or how his team would get their intel. "We think the group is planning something big, and when we know more, we'll probably want to put agents in your home."

"As long as you keep my family safe, I'll do what I can to stop this bullshit. Just let me know."

"Thanks. I'll be in touch." Drager gave him the number of an agent in the cyber-theft unit and hung up. Finding the money wasn't his focus, thankfully. But if the tech guys were successful, and the cyber trail led to Luke Maddox and the inner circle, it was one more charge to nail them on. Which one of the group had the hacking skills to pull off that kind of cyber theft? It hadn't really been a bank hack though, only a phone scam and email interception. A fairly low-tech phishing job. How many more politicians were at risk? Drager emailed their PR person, asking her to send out a warning. What next? He remembered the homicide meeting and jumped up. The drive to the District One building wasn't far, but if traffic was bad, it could take a while.

The MPD's homicide unit operated out of an old grade school across the street from tenement apartments, stretched out in a single level like army barracks. A group of young men in baggy pants watched him get out of his car and walk around to the front of the building. Inside, he approached the counter and showed the station clerk his badge. "I need to see Sergeant Murphy. He's expecting me."

"I think he's in a meeting." The uniformed clerk had a light southern accent.

"I know. I'm supposed to attend."

"All right, then. Step over to that door, and I'll let you in. The conference room is down a ways and on the right."

Drager stepped through the security door and checked his watch. He was right on time. He hurried into the meeting. Five men in suits and one woman sat at a rectangular table. She looked up, and he flinched. Jocelyn, his ex-wife! Technically, they were still married, but the paperwork had been filed. He hadn't known she was on Murphy's homicide team, and seeing her rattled him. She looked startled too, with that tight-lipped expression he knew so well. He nodded at Jocelyn, then glanced around at the others. "Agent Ross Drager. Sorry I'm late."

"You're not. We started early." Sergeant Murphy, at the end, looked tall even seated—and physically fit.

Drager sucked in his stomach. One of the reasons Jocelyn had lost interest in him was that he'd let himself go soft. But so had she, so it wasn't fair. As soon as he eased into a chair, he let his stomach muscles relax. As the detectives introduced themselves, he turned to each one, but his blind spot kept him from really seeing the man on his left. Drager noted all their names, but didn't tuck them away in his memory. All he needed was an update on the judge's homicide. Did anyone here know he was Jocelyn's ex-husband? She would probably tell her boss after the meeting, but it shouldn't matter.

Murphy stood and went to the whiteboard. "This is the list of ex-cons Bidwell put away who have the highest probability of coming after him." Ten names, none of which he could read at this distance.

"What criteria did you use?" he asked.

"History of violence, recent contact with the judge, and a record of making threats." Murphy stared at him. "Anyone you want to add?"

Drager hesitated. This situation was tricky, but he owed them some honesty. "Luke Maddox. Bidwell sentenced him to ten years for marijuana distribution when he was only eighteen."

The sergeant raised an eyebrow. "That describes a lot of people in prison. Has your suspect threatened the judge?"

"Indirectly. He's an activist for judicial reform." Drager couldn't give them anything else without compromising his own operation.

Murphy added Maddox's name to the list. "What else did we find?" The sergeant looked at the man to his left. Detective Harris.

"I finally talked to Bidwell's wife. She says the judge parked in that garage every Wednesday evening, then walked across the street to a poker game at the DownLow. Anyone who knew him or his routine could have been waiting."

"We need to question everyone who sat at the poker table with him." Murphy pointed at Harris. "Follow up." The sergeant called on the next man at the table. "Tell us about the autopsy."

"Bludgeoned from behind with a tire iron. At least four blows, one likely made when he was on the ground."

"What about the assailant?" Murphy sounded impatient.

The detective glanced at his notes. "Five eight or nine, about the same height as the victim. That's about all the ME could infer. No defense wounds. No trace evidence."

Murphy noted the suspect's height on the board.

"The techs found traces of soil on the cement near the body," another investigator added. "And from behind a support post, where the assailant probably waited."

"What about phone and financial records?" Murphy asked.

The other two detectives gave updates but offered no actionable information. Drager was ready to leave.

"Larson, what's happening with your case?" Murphy looked at Drager's ex.

Jocelyn straightened, bristling at being called Larson. He knew she hated that. Her throaty voice was always calm though, a smooth surface over a fiery passion. "The victim had someone else's ID, a prostitute's. I didn't know until I took the wrong relative to the morgue. Now I'm trying to figure out who she really is."

"Did you try facial recognition software?" Drager asked.

"Of course. But the victim was shot in the face, so it's not easy. As best I can determine, she isn't in our criminal database, but I'll search public and government files next."

Drager nodded at her. Jocelyn was tenacious about cases, even when she didn't want to be. She would ID the dead woman and find her killer. She always did. But why wasn't she working the judge's case? Now that he knew she was on Murphy's team, he'd skip the drive across town and just call her instead.

"When did she die?" he asked, not sure why he even cared. Was it just an excuse to talk to Jocelyn? They'd parted amicably but hadn't spoken since Kyle left for college. With a sudden longing, he realized he missed her. Even her bossy ways.

Surprised, Jocelyn blinked, then said, "The autopsy is tomorrow morning, but a tech at the scene thought she was probably killed last Tuesday or Wednesday."

"Send me her photo, and I'll check our databases," he offered.

"Thanks."

The sergeant's phone rang next to him on the table, and he glanced at it. "I have to take this." Murphy stepped out of the room.

Drager again thought to leave, but Jocelyn asked, "What's the bureau's interest in the judge's murder?"

"It may overlap with a case we're working. The activist group I mentioned."

"I thought JRN was targeting politicians."

She was always well informed. "They are, but we're covering all the bases."

Murphy stepped back in. "Someone from the U.S. Attorney's office will be joining our task force." He made a noise in his throat. "They had been investigating Judge Bidwell and had planned to charge him with racketeering, among other things. For the last ten years that he was on the bench in Virginia, he took bribes from Corrections for a Safer America in exchange for lengthy sentences."

"Holy shit!" Jocelyn was the first to respond.

"That's a private prison system, right?" Detective Harris asked.

Murphy nodded. "They're investigating the company too."

"How does this affect our case?" Harris wanted to know.

Murphy grimaced. "It means there are hundreds more people with a motive to kill Bidwell."

A long moment with only the hum of traffic outside.

Finally, Jocelyn asked, "Who knew about the investigation and the bribes?"

"We don't know yet."

Drager's thoughts came back to his target. Luke Maddox made a point of being informed about the judicial system and probably knew about the charges. But Drager couldn't mention him again. Sergeant Murphy might get overeager and try to bring Maddox in for questioning, which could produce nothing for their murder investigation, but might send Maddox farther underground. And possibly endanger their UC agent. Drager rubbed his throbbing eyes. They might never nail Maddox for the murder, so he needed Dallas to come through with a major crime setup.

Chapter 17

Tuesday, Oct. 7, 2:15 p.m.
Jocelyn searched the MPD's missing persons database, paging through screen after screen and trying not to grind her teeth. They were all young women, and many were blond. Analyzing their faces didn't help much. Her victim had been left nearly unrecognizable. The day before, after realizing she had the wrong ID, Jocelyn had gone into the cold room at the morgue and spent a few minutes staring at the dead woman's face for points of recognition. She'd focused on three: narrow chin, high hairline, and a tiny mole near the left ear. Now she was trying to find those features in a sea of faces. And trying not to think about the missing women as she scrolled through, because that could be devastating.

So far, none of the faces matched her three points. Jocelyn downed the last of her now-warm Mountain Dew, heaved a sigh, and opened the federal missing persons website. This could take hours, and she was on her own. Her partner was still out sick with the flu, and the rest of her team was working Judge Bidwell's murder, tracking down hundreds of ex-cons with a grudge.

Her phone rang, and she hesitated to pick up. The homicide department had to respond to every death in the

DC area, regardless of the circumstances. Totally inefficient. She couldn't afford to waste time on an accidental death that didn't need investigating. She'd let another team member take it . . . if they were in the building. After a minute, the message light came on, so she listened to the voicemail. Ross, her ex: "Hey, Jocelyn. Give me a call, so we can talk shop." How odd to suddenly have him in her life again, even on a work-only basis. She didn't have time to chat with him, but she remembered his offer to help her identify the shooting victim, so she returned his call.

He picked immediately. "Drager here."

"It's Jocelyn. How are you?" Why had she asked that? This wasn't a personal call.

"Lonely. I miss you."

His voice, those words. He might as well have reached out and squeezed her heart. She finally found her own voice. "It's been a long, strange two months. So it was a nice surprise to see you earlier."

"For me too."

An awkward silence.

Unsure of her feelings or what any of this meant, she got back to business. "Did you have a question for me? Or have any luck with your facial recognition software?"

"Not yet. Will you update me if your team gets any leads on Bidwell's murder?"

"Sure enough." Jocelyn recalled what he'd said about overlapping cases and wanted to know more. "Can you tell me what your real interest is in Luke Maddox? I won't share it with the team."

"He's an activist we have our eyes on. That's all I can say."

"I understand. I've gotta go. Bye." She hung up before he could respond. After being frustrated with their marriage for years and finally breaking away, why was she suddenly feeling pulled back in? Lonely, that was all. She needed to start dating. The thought almost made her laugh. Where did a middle-aged woman of color, who was also a cop, meet someone appropriate?

She turned back to her monitor, keyed *Maryland* into the search field, and started scanning. There were fewer blonds and more minorities in the national database, but no one matching her victim. She tried *Virginia* next. The fourth image caught her attention. High hairline and narrow chin. She couldn't see the mole, but it was on the side of the victim's face, so that didn't mean anything. Callie Sayers, thirty-one, of Fredericksburg, Virginia. If this was the dead woman, what was she doing in DC? A dozen reasons came to mind—shopping, theater, and political meetings, to name a few. Jocelyn scanned the brief report. Callie Sayers worked in Richmond and had been reported missing Thursday by her mother, Viola Sayers.

Protocol would be to inform the local police department first and see what they knew or thought about the disappearance, but she might get the runaround and didn't have time for jurisdictional bullshit. Jocelyn braced herself and called the mother's number.

After the second ring, an anxious voice asked, "Who's calling?"

"Detective Jocelyn Larson, Metro Police Department in DC. Is this Viola Sayers?"

A panicked breath. "Yes. Is this about Callie?"

"Possibly. Can you tell me what your daughter was wearing when she disappeared?" That had been too blunt, but she was already a week behind on this case.

"Why? Is she dead?" The woman choked back fear.

"I know this is difficult, but I'm trying to identify a murder victim."

"She was murdered? Oh no. My poor baby."

Lord, she hated this part. "We don't know if it's Callie yet. Tell me what she was wearing Tuesday."

"She doesn't live with me, so I didn't see her before she left to go into the capital. I don't know what she was wearing, but she always dressed nice." A pause while she collected herself. "I gave her picture to the local police."

"I know. I'm looking at it online. But the victim was shot in the face, so I can't say for sure." An image of the woman's body in the morgue displayed in Jocelyn's brain. "The victim had a tiny mole near her left ear, a pockmark in the V of her chest, and breasts of different sizes."

A pause, then wracking sobs.

She'd identified her victim. "I'm so sorry for your loss. Do you need a minute?"

"For what?" the woman cried. "If she's dead, nothing's ever gonna be the same."

"I want to find her killer, and I need your help. Can I ask a few questions?"

"Not right now." Mrs. Sayers hung up.

Jocelyn didn't blame her. What was her next move? The victim lived in Fredericksburg and worked in Richmond. The first was an hour's drive south, and the Virginia capital was an hour beyond that. It was too late to head out now, especially after a week of night shift and no days off. She would visit both places tomorrow after a good night's sleep.

Chapter 18

Tuesday, Oct. 7, 1:27 p.m.

Dallas twisted to free herself from the guard's grip, but he slammed her against the metal door. Pain enraged her, and she brought up a knee to plant in his balls. But she was off balance and not fast enough. He stepped back and drew his gun, aiming it at her head.

"Get on your knees!"

Oh shit! She had no choice. This wasn't her cause, and she wasn't going to die for it. Dallas dropped down. Maybe she could talk her way out of this. Or maybe she'd end up in jail. But the inner circle would probably bail her out. They had a plan and money in the bank for such situations. If they didn't, the bureau would. She breathed deeply and tried to calm herself.

"Hands on your head."

Again, she complied, as the guard radioed for help. She remembered the damn meth in her pocket and cursed herself for not ditching it earlier. The bail for drug possession would be considerably higher than for trespassing or B&E. Would the bureau fire her or demote her for it? No, of course not. UCs who infiltrated gangs often did drugs with their targets. That was how they built trust. She would get through this. Besides, the ID she had wasn't her real name.

"What are you doing here?" the guard asked.

"Nothing. I came to protest the governor's speech like everyone else out there. Then I got bored and wandered inside."

"This area is locked. How did you get in?"

"I just walked in."

He shook his head. "Why did you run from me?"

"I got scared. I thought you were going to arrest me." She gave a timid smile. "I'm just a college student with ideals, and I've never been in trouble before. Please let me go."

His face twitched with indecision, and the gun dropped a few inches. "Show me what's in your pockets."

Oh hell. Drugs and lock-picks. She couldn't empty them. "Come on. I'm no threat to anyone. Just let me go."

"Shut up. I'm putting you under citizen's arrest." Despite his raised volume, he sounded uncertain. With one hand, he reached to his belt and unsnapped a pair of handcuffs. "Stand up and turn around."

"Will you cuff me in front, please? It's less painful." She knew from training exercises when she'd played the unsub.

"It's not protocol."

Damn. Dallas turned around and put her hands back. This guy was nervous, and nervous people with guns were unpredictable. He cuffed her and led her to the security office in a back corner of the building. Once they were in private, he searched her pockets and pulled out the lock-picks and bag of meth.

"A thief and a druggie." The guard grinned and shook his head.

She couldn't tell if he was pleased or disgusted. He pushed her toward a chair, then walked out, taking her things with him.

Dallas sat on the hard wooden chair and waited. This would be a long day, or couple of days. Had Abby and Aaron completed their mission? Or had everyone fled when the alarm went off?

Forty minutes later, a DC police officer showed up, put a new pair of cuffs on her, and led her to his patrol car, parked in a handicapped space in front of the building. The protestors had cleared out, and the street scene was calm and normal. Everyone but her had gone home.

Over the next three hours, she was strip-searched, fingerprinted, and booked into custody. She was also shouted at, ink-stamped with a number on her am, and handled like a possession rather than a person. Every step of the process was degrading, but particularly the strip search. Having a stranger shove a finger in her ass to check for drugs was the worst. How did criminals and addicts cope with it? Some people cycled in and out of jail on a regular basis and were subjected to the ordeal with every lockup. Did they start to feel less human?

The female officer gave her clothes back, minus the pocket contents, and Dallas pulled them on, relieved not to be naked any longer in this hostile place. "Can I make a phone call now?" The fact that she hadn't been given a pair of jail scrubs meant she might be released after an arraignment soon.

"Not until the charges are filed, and you missed the afternoon court session." The officer, who outweighed her by fifty pounds, didn't make eye contact.

"Oh come on. It's your decision. I need to let people know where I am."

"It's the rules. Step this way."

The jail officer walked her past smaller holding cells filled to capacity to a big area with dirty gray, peeling paint. Benches lined the walls and filled the center. About fifteen women occupied the room, most in their early twenties. Some were obviously prostitutes, and others had the telltale signs of drug use: skin lesions, brittle hair, and no body fat. Two women, both in their late thirties, wore layers of clothing, as if they were homeless. Everyone else was probably dealing with a money issue—theft, fraud, or failure to pay the court.

A dozen pairs of eyes looked over to see the new detainee, but most turned away just as quickly. One young woman, sporting a shaved head with a bandana tied around it, kept her eyes on Dallas as she took a seat on the floor next to the wall. Even in the dim light, Dallas wanted to be able to see everyone at once—in case one of the meth addicts in withdrawal came at her in misguided rage. This would be a sleepless night. The best she could hope for was an early morning arraignment, with bail set low.

A few hours later, a woman on the bench next to her was released, and Dallas took her space. The steel bench was slightly less uncomfortable than the concrete floor, and eventually she was able to lie down for a while. For short periods throughout the night she drifted off, but was awakened repeatedly by the clanging of the doors as women were brought in and out. Thirst finally drove Dallas to vacate her spot long enough to sip water from the rusty drinking faucet. She hoped to avoid the toilet in the corner. Listening to others use it was bad enough.

Time stretched into eternity, and her bones ached from the pressure of the hard bench and inactivity. But there was no room to pace. One of the middle-age homeless women occasionally walked back and forth in her own tight space, mumbling to herself, but it annoyed everyone when she did. The crowded room had to be a nightmare for anyone who was claustrophobic, antisocial, or anxiety prone.

Dallas tried to stay focused on her case, thinking through scenarios and next steps. But in the early hours of the morning, she gave up and replayed fond memories of travel and adventures she'd taken. She remembered one excursion during high school with her Aunt Lynn, who'd taken her to Florida on one of her research trips. After growing up in Flagstaff, Dallas had loved the beaches, the warm winter sun, and the bright colors everywhere. If not for her aunt, her childhood would have been a lot worse. Without the acting lessons, language workshops, and a host of other keep-her-busy activities, she wouldn't have the skills and confidence to handle undercover assignments. She might have ended up following in her parents' troubled footsteps and spending a lot of time in jails like this one.

Her mother, perpetually jealous of Aunt Lynn's success, had sometimes refused to give Dallas permission to participate. Drunk and belligerent, Roxy had fought with her sister about taking Dallas to Florida. Aunt Lynn had simply ignored her sister, bought the ticket, and told Dallas to pack and be ready. By fifteen, she no longer cared what her parents thought. They had shuffled her from one relative to another while they partied and blew what little money they had. Her father had been prone to fistfights and had landed in jail a few times while she was still in grade school. This was the first time she really understood what that experience had been like for him. Now that he'd died of liver failure, her heart had softened, and visualizing him being treated like a non-human tugged at her emotions.

Heavy footsteps caught her attention and made her sit up quickly. A big woman with thick arms and a giant head loomed over her. "Get yo' ass up! It's my turn on the bench."

Oh hell, she didn't need this. The angry inmate was even bigger than the guard, maybe two-fifty. Dallas decided to give up the space. But she didn't move fast enough. The woman reached down, grabbed her hair, and yanked.

The bitch! Dallas reacted without thinking. She shot to her feet, going in the same direction as the woman's pull, while landing an undercut to her solar plexus. The combined forces knocked the woman back, and she let go of Dallas' hair. But the inmate didn't give up. She hauled herself up and came at Dallas, head down, trying to ram her. Dallas stepped aside, but the space between them was small, and the big woman caught her on the hip. Dallas' body flew back, her knees buckled against the end of the bench, and her head slammed into the concrete wall. *Fuck!* The pain enraged her, and she pushed to her feet, fearing another onslaught.

The doors clanged and a guard shouted, "Stop or I'll taser you both!"

The big woman came at her anyway, aiming to land a roundhouse punch to her face. Dallas ducked enough to take the blow on her cheek instead of her nose. But the knuckle on bone was excruciating.

The guard crossed the room and shoved her stun gun against the other inmate's back. Her assailant blinked, cried out, and spun around. The guard zapped her in the chest, hitting the charge again and again until the giant woman finally dropped to her knees.

Dallas had already stepped back, hoping to avoid getting shocked.

Another guard, a male, came into the holding area. "You should have put Aussie in a cell by herself." He grabbed the big woman by one arm. The female guard grabbed the other, and they led the stunned inmate out of the holding area.

A young detainee near the door laughed. "Big dumb fuck."

Dallas breathed a sigh of relief.

"Hey, you're bleeding." A woman on a nearby bench pointed to her head.

Dallas reached up to her cheek, but it was dry. The side of her head where she'd hit the wall was sticky though. Grimacing with pain, she shuffled over to the toilet area, grabbed the last few tissues on the roll, and held them to her wound. *Damn,* this place reeked.

When Dallas sat back down, the woman who'd mentioned the blood scooted next to her. She was older than the others, with short, ragged hair and lines around her mouth. Her dark skin shimmered with sweat. "What are you in for?" she asked. "A pretty white girl like you?"

"Trespassing." Mentioning the drugs was unnecessary.

The woman scoffed. "You'll get released after your arraignment."

"I hope so." Surprising herself, Dallas asked her name.

"Mona." Her voice quivered. "I won't be so lucky. I always get lost in the system."

With time to kill, Dallas decided to hear her story. "How so?"

"My first arrest was in New York when I was sixteen. They accused me of mugging some white guy." Mona shook her head. "They just grabbed the nearest black person and hauled me off. They had no witnesses and no case against me, but I spent three years on Rikers Island—or Rikers Hell, as I like to call it—waiting for a trial." The woman shook her head, her voice resigned and weary. "They pressured me again and again to plead guilty and take a deal, but I wouldn't. Finally, the DA admitted he had no case, and the charges were dismissed. Three fucking years of my life. I was just a kid! So I never finished high school."

"I've heard horror stories about Rikers Island, but that's insane."

"They're all true. And it's hell for the young kids out there. After they put me in solitary for two months, I tried to kill myself. I thought I would starve or go crazy. It fucked me up. I have anxiety and flashbacks, and I can't seem to fit in anywhere. So I live on the streets and do odd jobs to get by."

"You could probably sue the prison."

Mona let out a sad laugh and shook her head. "Nobody cares about me."

Dallas was trying to stay in character and didn't know what else to say. How did shit like that happen? If Mona's parents had put their teenage daughter in a room by herself for twenty-three hours a day with nothing to do and very little food, they would have been arrested for abuse. But it was somehow okay for the state to treat her that way. Dallas couldn't let herself listen to any more of Mona's story. She was on assignment and had to keep her head clear and focused. Becoming too sympathetic with her targets could undermine her effectiveness. But boy, did they have a point.

She got up and walked in place for a while to get her blood flowing. She needed some ice to put on her face, which had started to throb, but that wasn't going to happen. What the hell time was it, anyway?

Chapter 19

After another long stretch of time, it was finally morning, and two new female officers came into the room. One of them called out three inmate names, including Tara Adams. Dallas sat up.

"Time for court. Use the toilet now if you need to."

Oh hell. Her bladder hurt too much to wait. An inmate whistled as Dallas pulled down her pants, but she didn't care anymore. At least she was getting out of this room.

"What about me?" Mona yelled. "I've been in here for days."

The guards ignored her, put handcuffs on the three who'd been called, and escorted them out. They went downstairs, through another maze of hallways, and outside to a secluded area where a small bus waited. The morning sun on her skin was glorious—for a brief thirty seconds—then Dallas climbed on the bus, headed for an arraignment.

The courtroom was packed with handcuffed men, some in prison scrubs and some in street clothes. Several security officers stood in back. One by one, the inmates were called before the judge, an older woman with oversized glasses. A clerk read the charges, and the people in handcuffs entered a plea. Dallas couldn't help but notice that most of the prisoners were black. Except three of the men, and one of them was Latino. Her turn came, and the charges surprised her: breaking and entering, possession of burglary tools, trespassing, and resisting arrest. No drugs? What the hell? Had someone pocketed them along the way? She felt almost giddy with relief. The rest of the list was a familiar tactic. Charge a suspect with everything you could think of, then pressure them to plead guilty to the most important offense by offering to drop the rest.

"How do you plead?" The judge peered over her glasses, staring, as if Dallas were an alien. She had barely looked at the other inmates who'd stood before her.

"Not guilty."

"Can you afford an attorney? If not, one will be appointed for you."

"No." As a ghostwriter, Tara Adams couldn't. Defense attorneys charged two to four hundred an hour.

"Bail is set at twenty thousand. Your next court date is November fifth. Do not miss it."

Damn. Dallas hoped the inner circle could afford two thousand for a bail bondsman to get her out. They seemed to have money for adventures, but she'd overhead Luke and Abby talking about their main benefactor pulling support, so they might not want to spend the cash. Dallas went back to her place on the bench and waited through another round of pleas.

Unless the bureau made her charges go away, eventually the Virginia court would issue a no-show warrant for Tara Adams' arrest—when she didn't come back. Her photo was now in the criminal database too. Dallas had darkened her hair to dirty blond for this assignment and wore heavy makeup, especially around her eyes, but none of that would fool facial recognition software—if anyone ever did a comparison. As long as she kept out of the news and off social media, her cover wouldn't be blown.

Seven hours after leaving, she arrived back at the jail, and the three female inmates were split up. One seemed to be headed back to the holding area, and another was led upstairs, where the main long-stay cells were located. Dallas was escorted to the in-take room where she'd been processed. Yet another female guard pointed at the wooden chair. "Wait here." She moved toward the door.

Dallas didn't sit. Whatever was happening made her nervous. "I want to make a phone call."

"You don't need to. You made bail. I'm getting your things."

Hallelujah!

An hour later, she stood outside the back entrance of the jail, looking around for the van or Luke's truck. All she had in her pockets were her phony driver's license and her cell phone. The twenty-dollar bill she'd brought along, in case of a scenario like this one, was gone, and so were her lock-picks and lucky cloth. She'd been too embarrassed to even ask what happened to it. Knowing the keepsake was gone forever gave her a low-level anxiety. Yet, she felt strangely liberated as well. Someone had stolen the packet of meth too, and for that, she was so grateful she considered the other items a fair trade. She desperately needed a shower, a meal, and a toothbrush, but she felt giddy anyway.

A middle-aged woman in large sunglasses approached her. "Tara Adams?"

"Yes."

"I'm with JRN, and I paid your bail. Your ride is waiting

for you two blocks that way." She pointed left.

"Thank you."

"You're welcome, but it wasn't my money. I'm just a delivery woman. Now go get back to work, fighting for the cause."

"I'm on my way." Dallas nodded and jogged down the street. She would have liked five minutes alone to find a public phone and call Drager, but she was too relieved to care that much.

Dallas spotted the white van at a gas station. Both front seats were occupied. *Damn.* Abby had come along. Dallas climbed in the side door and sank into the bench seat, relieved to be getting the hell out of Richmond.

"I'm so happy to see you both," Dallas said. "Thanks for bailing me out."

Abby turned in her seat and narrowed her eyes. "We have a problem."

Chapter 20

Wednesday, Oct. 8, 9:30 a.m.
With a can of Mountain Dew in hand and a blueberry muffin on the dashboard, Jocelyn took the I-95 ramp and headed south. She crossed into Virginia soon after without any fanfare. State lines didn't mean much to commuters in this area, but she was officially out of her jurisdiction now. She'd spent the first half of her childhood in North Carolina, then moved to Maryland in high school when her father got a job with the government. She'd always lived in the suburbs because downtown DC was too expensive, and because she liked to have a yard with a grill and some sunflowers. So driving took a chunk out of her life every day, and she sometimes listened to e-books, mostly biographies, but she'd also recently enjoyed a sci-fi series called *Wool.*

A thick, lush band of trees lined the road, with hints of red and yellow in the leaves, and a high cloud cover gave the sky a bluish-silver tone. Overall, a pleasant fall day for a drive. Instrumental soul music played softly, letting her mind roam freely. Her thoughts kept drifting to Ross. It had been such a surprise to see him at the meeting yesterday, followed by his call. *But that had been mostly business,* she told herself. She was an asset to him at the moment, that was all. That was how the bureau operated. They cultivated people and used them. It annoyed her that Ross wouldn't share details about his investigation into Luke Maddox.

They used to share their cases with each other—sometimes. More often, after a long day of focusing on crime, they'd wanted to talk about anything else. Or simply be alone with their books or TV programs. Nothing specific had gone wrong with their relationship. They'd simply gotten on each other's nerves, then lost their sexual spark and drifted apart. Once Kyle was gone, they'd known it was over, but she had been the one to say it out loud. Seeing Ross yesterday had stirred up old feelings. She hadn't wanted to admit it, but why else was he on her mind? Why else did she keep reaching for her phone to call him? Had they made a mistake? The divorce wasn't final yet.

Jocelyn let it go and played out how she would question Viola Sayers and anyone else she could round up. She also had to search Callie Sayers' home, which could be the original crime scene. Someone, maybe a new boyfriend, could have shot her after a fight, transported her to DC, then dumped her. *Not a chance.* Callie's mother had mentioned that her daughter had left for the capital. Where she was going and who she planned to see was the critical, still-missing information.

Finally, a road sign indicated she was only five miles from the Fredericksburg exit. Jocelyn shut off her music, finished her muffin, and focused on the road.

The Sayers lived in a modest house in a pleasant suburb with shade trees and tidy lawns, a reminder that living the good life didn't insulate anyone from crime. Three cars filled the long driveway, with another parked on the street. Family and friends had gathered to comfort the grieving parents. Was Mr. Sayers in the picture? There was so much she still didn't know about the victim or her circumstances. Mrs. Sayers hadn't answered her phone that morning, so she'd been unable to get any details. Jocelyn parked and walked up the driveway. By the time she reached the front door, it was open.

A man in his mid-twenties gave her a once-over. "Are you a cop?" His eyes were swollen and his hair rumpled, as if he'd run his hands through it.

"Detective Larson, DC police." This far south, they might not know that *Metro* meant the capital. "Who are you?"

"Roan Sayers." After a hesitation, he held out his hand.

Jocelyn shook it. "I'd like to talk to the family."

"Come on in."

She followed him across a foyer. "Are you Callie's brother?"

"Yes, ma'am. I'm supposed to be in class today, but how could I? My mother is beside herself. We all are."

They stepped into a family room with closed shades. Three women sat on a floral couch watching family videos. The youngest cried quietly. The older woman looked up, reached for the remote, and shut off the TV.

"This is Detective Larson," the brother said.

The mother stood. "I'm Viola. Forgive me for being rude last night."

"It's understandable."

One of the other women stood. She looked like a younger version of Viola. "I have to run, but I'll be back around supper time with lasagna." She hugged Mrs. Sayers.

Jocelyn stepped toward her and pulled a notepad out of her pocket. "I'd like your name and phone number please. We may need to talk later."

"Ruby Davison. I'm Callie's aunt. But I have no idea what I

can tell you about this shocking tragedy." Ruby shook her head but wrote the information down anyway. Jocelyn walked her to the door to see which car she left in, but she knew none of this would matter. Gut instinct told her Callie's murder wasn't connected to her family. A boyfriend or a one-night stand gone badly would be the obvious leads. But the gunshots to her face and the wrong ID pointed to something more complicated. A perp who knew the victim and had the time to plan his attack—or possibly a serial killer.

Back in the family room, she pulled a chair from the desk and sat in front of the family. The younger woman leaned toward her. "I'm Devon Fairchild, Callie's older sister. Please tell us what happened to her."

"I don't know much yet, except that she was shot sometime Tuesday or Wednesday, and her body was left at a construction site." The family would learn about the dumpster eventually, but there was no need for them to visualize it now when their grief was so raw. "Callie is in the morgue at the new forensics building in DC. They're doing the autopsy today, so she'll be released after that." Jocelyn was still waiting on a call from the ME.

"Do we have to pick her up?" The brother looked disturbed by the idea.

"A local funeral home will likely transport her for you." The family needed more from her, but all she had were questions. "When was the last time you saw Callie?" Pen in hand, Jocelyn looked at Mrs. Sayers first. She would have to put an initial by each note to indicate which family member gave the information. Typically, she would never question more than one family member at a time, but she was on her own and had to access everyone she could while she had the opportunity. The two-hour round-trip drive demanded it.

This was probably just her first trip down, but her partner had promised to come in the next day, and she would let him do some of the legwork.

"Last Sunday. Callie had dinner here with all of us, like we do most weeks." Mrs. Sayers gripped a handkerchief in her lap. "Except when Roan works weekends."

"Did either of you see her after that?" Jocelyn glanced back and forth at the siblings.

"No." They spoke in unison.

"But I talked to her Monday," Devon said. "Callie mentioned taking some time off and going to DC for a couple of days. She had a benefit dinner Tuesday night and a date with some guy on Wednesday."

"What benefit?"

"I don't know. She told me, but I don't remember."

"It's important." Jocelyn glanced at the mother. "Do you know?"

"Not really." She looked down at her callused hands. "Callie was good-hearted and involved in a lot of causes."

"Like what?"

"Homeless veterans was her biggest thing," Roan said. "Her fiancé was a military sergeant, so she belonged to a group of war widows."

A charitable cause seemed like the wrong track. "What about her date? Do you know the guy's name?"

They all shook their heads. Finally, Mrs. Sayers said, "It was the first time she mentioned a guy since Dave died. She said they were just friends and changed the subject. I didn't want to pry."

Jocelyn decided to move on. Now that she knew the victim's name, she could get phone and credit card records and retrace her last moments. The mystery date would surface. "What did Callie drive?" The car had to be somewhere—with her purse and the ticket to whatever event she'd attended. Maybe even her cell phone.

"A red Chevy Cruze."

Jocelyn made notes, planning to call MPD dispatch with the description as soon as she walked out the door. "Can you think of anyone who would want to kill her?"

"No!" The sister was loudest. "Callie was a sweetheart."

"Do you have a key to her home? I need to see the place."

"She keeps one outside by the back door. It's under a clay pot." Mrs. Sayers let out a little sob. "I went over there Wednesday night when she didn't return any of my calls."

Jocelyn needed to know more about the victim's friends. "Where did she work?"

"The district courthouse in Richmond. She was a clerk."

That opened up a whole new can of worms. "Did any defendants ever threaten her? Was she afraid of anyone?"

Mrs. Sayers shook her head. "I don't think so. She was just a clerk, not a judge or a lawyer."

Jocelyn decided to stop at the court after searching the victim's house. Or come back tomorrow if she ran out of time. "Who was her boss?"

"Judge Oswald." Mrs. Sayers suddenly got up. "Where are my manners? Would you like some iced tea?"

"Thanks, but I'll get going." Jocelyn stood too. "How long had Callie worked at the courthouse?"

"About ten years." The grieving mother started for the kitchen. "Most of that time, she clerked for Judge Bidwell, but he retired last year."

Bidwell? The murdered judge who'd died a day or so after Callie was her ex-boss? Adrenaline rushed up Jocelyn's spine.

Chapter 21

Jocelyn found the key under the clay pot and shook her head. Why did people make it so easy to break into their homes? The backyard of Callie Sayers' cottage wasn't even fenced off from the street. She unlocked the sliding-glass door and started to step in. A sudden sound in the house made her pull her weapon. Who the hell was in there? Had the killer come back to cover his tracks? Both hands on her Glock, Jocelyn stepped cautiously into the small dining area and glanced around. To her left, an empty kitchen, and straight ahead, a living room. No blood, no disarray, no sign of a shooting or struggle. The smell of rotting garbage distracted her for a second, then she took three steps toward the center of the home.

Another thump, like two boards banging together. Jocelyn spun left, focusing on a door leading out of the kitchen. The sound had come from the garage. She crossed the narrow strip of vinyl and yanked open the door. "Police!"

The cluttered garage seemed empty. Something small and dark scurried from behind a stack of boxes and made a beeline for a cat door on the outside wall. But it wasn't a cat. A raccoon? Jocelyn's heart rate slowed and she lowered her gun. She felt a little silly for shouting "police" at a rodent, but hey, that kind of pre-emptive move had kept her alive in a dangerous job. But if there was a cat door, where was the cat? A glance around the garage indicated nothing obvious that needed to be searched—yet. Basics first.

Back inside the house, she started to look for a computer, where she might find everything she needed. The victim's cell phone would be a better source, but she suspected it was in the district's landfill by now. The killer had gone to a whole lot of trouble to obscure Callie's identity. He may have even hidden her car, but at least now Jocelyn had a make and model for patrol officers to watch for. It was tempting to start thinking of the judge as the killer, but it was only suspicion. She had to find something solid.

The small living room was so tidy it looked more like a display than a living space. No magazines, coasters, or even a remote was visible. She pulled on gloves and opened the single drawer on the end table to check for a remote to see if the victim had one. It was there, along with a tube of hand lotion. That was it. Callie Sayers hadn't spent much time in her living room, even though she had a nice flat-screen TV in the corner.

Jocelyn moved on to the first room off the short hallway, shocked at the difference. Desk drawers left open, papers on the floor, and plastic storage tubs pulled out of the closet with the lids off. Someone had searched this room—but for what? She trotted back to the living room and checked the front door and windows. All locked with no signs of forced entry. The shooter could have kept the victim's keys long enough to let himself in.

Returning to the little office, she discovered a monitor and a mouse on the desk but no computer. *Damn.* Either Callie had taken her laptop with her when she traveled to the city, or the killer had come here after her death and stolen it.

She would have to get a forensics team down here to dust for fingerprints and collect trace evidence. If she never found the actual crime scene where Callie had been shot, this might be the only place the killer had left traces of himself. But this house was completely out of their jurisdiction, and she had no idea how the MPD would handle it. She'd never had a situation like it, and she planned to pass the responsibility to Sergeant Murphy and let him work through it.

The master bedroom had likely been searched too, but the perp had only focused on the dresser and nightstand, leaving some of the drawers slightly ajar. The closet seemed to have been undisturbed. Had he run out of time? She riffled through the dresser quickly, not finding anything but clothes. If there had been something significant, the perp had taken it. Jocelyn realized she was wasting her time. The technicians could cover this more thoroughly. Her effort would be better spent at the courthouse, asking questions of people who'd worked with Callie. The murder had to be connected to her job. Or more likely, to the judge she used to clerk for—who'd been charged with taking bribes. She checked her cell phone and realized that by the time she got to the court, it would be too late to find anyone still working. This investigation was no longer a simple *hooker shooting* and she needed help. The US Attorney's office might even take over the case. She needed to notify the local police to keep an eye on the house and call Sergeant Murphy with her update. But she could do both on the drive home.

Her phone rang, and she pulled it from her pocket. Was that the medical examiner's number? She took the call. "Detective Larson speaking."

"This is Anna Walz, assistant ME. You asked me to call when the autopsy was complete. I just emailed the report."

"Thanks. When was the time of death?"

"Tuesday evening, most likely between five and midnight. I know that's a wide window, but after a body's been dead a few days and left outside, that's the best we can do."

"I understand. Did you find anything significant I need to know? I'm in Fredericksburg at the victim's home."

"She was shot at close range and both bullets exited her head." A pause while a paper ruffled in the background. "One other odd thing. The victim had cigarette burns on the bottom of her feet. Her assailant tortured her before shooting her."

What the hell had Callie had that the killer wanted so badly?

Chapter 22

Wednesday, Oct. 8, 3:35 p.m.

As Luke started the van, Dallas braced herself. What the hell was Abby pissed about now? "Problem? What do you mean?"

"What happened to the meth? It wasn't listed in your charges, and Cree says you guys never made it to the governor's car." Abby's eyes blazed and her mouth twitched.

Oh hell. If she had ditched the packet, she would have faced this same scrutiny. But she'd taken the risk of hanging on to it to keep her cover, and it was still blowing up in her face. "I don't know. I was surprised when they read the charges and meth possession wasn't listed. Someone must have pocketed it."

"I find that hard to believe," Abby argued. "Cops in Virginia like to bust people for drugs."

Luke pulled the van into the street and didn't say anything.

Did he doubt her too? "I was stopped by a security guard, not a real cop, and he searched my pockets." Dallas wouldn't let Abby intimidate her. She didn't care if the bitch thought she'd chickened out—as long as no one started to think she was a fed. "Besides, the guard had plenty of other things to get excited about, such as the lock-picks I used to set off the alarm."

Abby shook her head. "I've heard of police planting drugs on detainees and stealing drugs from evidence lockers, but no one who gets busted with meth in their possession gets away with no charges."

"I was with Cree the whole time. You can ask him!" Dallas let herself get angry and raised her voice. "This is bullshit. I carried the damn drugs and took the risk, and now I'm facing a burglary charge. Not to mention spending the night on a cement floor and getting assaulted by a three-hundred-pound woman."

Luke finally glanced back. "Are you all right?"

"I've got a lump on the back of my head, a massive headache, and I haven't eaten since yesterday. But yeah, I'm fine." She needed Luke on her side and Abby to shut the hell up. It was time to ask. "I'd like to stop at my apartment, shower, and pick up a few more things. In fact, I want to get my car and drive it out to the farmhouse so I have access to it."

"No." Abby didn't even turn to face her.

"Why not? I think I've proven myself."

Abby scoffed. "You failed your mission and got arrested, and now you've put all of us in jeopardy."

Luke braked for traffic, then turned to Abby. "I told you to drop it. Tara stays with us." He made a left turn, clearly not heading toward Georgetown and her apartment.

"Can I get my car?" Feeling bitchy now, Dallas tried to find the balance between asserting her needs and pissing everyone off.

"Not now," Luke said. "It's not worth the argument. Everything is changing rapidly, and we'll have to make some group decisions after Friday."

Dallas let it go. "Can we stop for food? I'm starving."

"I have half a sandwich," Abby offered. "That should hold

you until we get home."

"I'll take it." Dallas reached for the sandwich. "Do you have water?"

Abby passed both requests back to her without commenting.

"After I eat this, I'm lying down to nap for a while. I'm exhausted." That was the truth. She felt like she could pass out. The ride home could be an opportunity to chat them up and find out what else they'd planned for Friday, but she was too tired to focus or retain information at the moment. After a quick snooze, she'd be ready to go again.

Dallas woke an hour later to the sound of heated voices. She heard Abby say, "I think she's a risk. How much do we even know about her?"

Dallas forced herself to focus, but kept her eyes closed.

Luke responded, "We know Tara supports our cause and is willing to take risks with us. That's all that matters. We're not kicking her out."

"What if the police come looking for her?"

"They'll go to her apartment in DC. I said to drop it."

Abby was quiet after that, so Dallas sat up. They were on the highway in Virginia, headed north. "Can we stop somewhere, please? I need to pee."

"We'll be home in half an hour," Luke said.

"I can't wait that long."

Abby cut in, "Let's go ahead and stop. I need to use the bathroom too, and you can run into the store for more beer."

Dallas sighed. She wouldn't get to call her contact with Abby in the store, but that was fine. She still needed more details about the Pearlman mission on Friday before she contacted Drager. When she had them, she'd find a way.

Chapter 23

Wednesday, Oct. 8, 6:05 p.m.

Luke tasted the pot of beef stew he'd just made and added more marjoram. Along with the cornbread Abby was baking, this meal was one of the few, besides pizza, that everyone in the group liked. Cree tended to be really picky about vegetables, and Abby had eclectic tastes. The timer on the oven sounded, and he reached over to shut it off. Abby came into the kitchen. "Are we ready?"

"Yep. Will you let everyone know?"

Abby turned and walked away without answering. She'd been distant and weird since he'd broken off with her, and now she was upset that yesterday's mission had failed to get the drugs planted in the governor's car. Abby had also wanted to leave Tara in jail, claiming it was too risky to be associated with her bail, but Luke hadn't even considered abandoning her. If they couldn't count on each other to help get out of jail, what was the point of the broader mission? Now he wondered if Abby could be a loyal and fully functional member. She seemed a little high-strung lately. She'd also insisted on going with him today so he couldn't be alone with Tara—a long uncomfortable trip.

The group gathered at the dining table, with everyone surprisingly quiet. Except Cree, who asked Tara about her time in jail, after sheepishly apologizing for leaving her behind to get caught. She described the assault from the other inmate—an experience Luke related to—but then seemed reluctant to share anything else. Luke understood that too. He held up his beer bottle for a toast. "To Tara, who took one for the team. We're glad to have you back."

"Thanks. But we failed our mission, so I don't get much credit."

"No, we didn't fail," Luke countered. "We may not have planted drugs on the governor like we wanted, but we got our message out there, and the Virginia media is now discussing the private-prison issue. I think public reaction to the transfer will be negative enough to shut it down." Maybe that was wishful thinking, but he was trying to cheer up Tara. She was facing some serious charges. "Have you decided how you're going to handle this? I can contact a lawyer for you." He was glad the JRN network was extensive and included a few law enforcement and government officials as well as professionals of every kind.

"It's tempting to just not show up for court," Tara said, between bites of stew. "How are they going to find me?"

Abby cut in. "The problem is that they're even looking." Her voice grew loud and trembled with emotion. "Now that the Virginia cops have Tara on their radar as an activist, it's a risk for the rest of us if she stays here. I think she should leave."

"No." Luke glared at his ex. "We don't abandon our members. And now that our funding has been cut off, we might have to move soon anyway. I still have to talk to Hana about that. In the meantime, Tara's no more of a risk than any of the rest of us."

Abby slammed down her knife. "I disagree."

"I'm with Luke," Cree said. "We all know the risks, and we could all go to prison."

"We can come back to this discussion after our mission Friday." Luke looked at Aaron. "Do we have Stella Pearlman's schedule yet?"

"She'll be out of the house between one and three."

"Perfect." This mission was bolder than anything they'd ever done, and it was happening fast. But the decriminalization vote was Friday, and they had to be proactive. He started to outline the plan. "We'll take several vehicles and park in different locations, in case we have to make a fast getaway and only have one exit route."

"But we're parking the van right out front, right?" Abby asked.

"Yes. Cree and I will wear blue jumpsuits and work belts, so we'll look like electricians." They had recently painted the *Eric's Electric* sign on the van so no one would pay attention to it. "Cree will disable the home's security, and we'll walk right in the front door." He touched Abby's hand to reassure her. "You'll be down the street, watching for us, ready to cause a distraction if necessary."

"I want to go in the house. Tara can be lookout."

Luke decided to let it go. He needed to placate Abby until he could find a way to ease her out. "Fine."

"I'll be on the other end of the block, monitoring the police scanner," Aaron said.

"What happens if the senator refuses to vote our way?" Abby asked. "His dog may not be as important to him as we think."

"He'll go along." Luke had been worried about that too, but now he had a backup plan that seemed foolproof. "The senator will not only vote with us, he'll bring in a few others.

And he'll never report the incident or call for a new vote."

Abby spun toward him. "Why not?"

"We'll have Pearlman's laptop. Tell them what you found, Aaron."

The analyst grinned. "Once I had remote access of his computer, I dug through his files and found some salacious photos. I'm sure the senator doesn't consider them to be child pornography, but the state of Maryland does."

Tara cocked her head. "What exactly are they?"

"Naked fourteen-year-old girls."

"Gotta love politicians." Tara laughed. "The hypocrite probably voted for stiffer sentencing for possessing such material. They never learn."

Cree chuckled too. "Like that congressman who pushed for drug-testing food stamp recipients, then was arrested for cocaine."

Luke could have added a dozen more examples, but he wanted to stay focused. "Let's run through the timing."

"Wait," Tara cut in. "What happens inside the house? You call Pearlman and threaten to hurt his dog? How do you prove you have the pup?"

"We'll send images, maybe a short video."

"What if he tells you to fuck off?"

"I'll bring up the laptop and threaten to expose him."

Tara smiled. "This could work. Do you really think the vote could pass?"

"It may not." Luke refused to let it bother him. "But having the head of the Congressional Judiciary Committee vote in favor will be a huge political win. Other politicians will get on board, and it will pass the next time. We have to start it rolling. In a punitive society, reform takes time."

Tara went back to eating stew, so everyone else did too.

Between mouthfuls, Luke outlined the timing of the day from the moment they left the house, then ran through some worst-case scenarios. Cree and Tara were the most concerned about the mission, and he did his best to reassure them. But he was worried too. If they were caught, they would face ten- or fifteen-year sentences, at least. It almost made him let out a bitter laugh. He'd served ten years for holding someone else's pot. He might actually be sentenced to less time for extortion. Many rapists had served less time, along with nearly everyone who committed manslaughter. He shook it off. He'd been through this in his head a million times. All he could do now was move forward and push for change.

After the dinner meeting, Abby and Aaron went back to their rooms, but Luke headed to the living area to check the news. Cree and Tara joined him. He turned on the TV and switched to CNN. As a group, they usually watched movies, particularly comedies or indie slice-of-life films, but they were all news junkies too and checked multiple sources every day. The newscaster spent ten minutes talking about the Ebola crisis, showing graphs of how quickly they thought it could spread, then switched to the daily drone strike report in the Middle East. Luke got up, intending to go check his email, when the pretty newscaster caught his attention:

"In a breaking development, a judge's murder in Washington DC may have a new, deeper new motive. Sources tell us that retired Judge J.D. Bidwell had been investigated for racketeering, fraud, and corruption. The charges, which had just been filed, indicate that during Bidwell's twenty-year seat on the circuit court in Virginia, he took more than two hundred payments from a company known as CSA, Corrections for a Safer America, a private-prison contractor that runs facilities around the country. In exchange for the payments, the US Attorney's office says Bidwell gave defendants maximum sentences, essentially selling them for profit."

The news landed like a punch in his gut. He'd been sold for cash? Ten years of his life stolen, so the judge could drive a better car or play golf in Hawaii? Luke collapsed back onto the couch.

The newscaster continued: "The payments amounted to more than two million dollars, and the IRS has frozen the judge's assets in an attempt to collect taxes on the money."

"Two million!" Cree's mouth dropped open.

"The scandal made us take a deeper look at the private-prison industry and how it operates," the newscaster said. "Almost all for-profit prison contracts include minimum quota clauses that stipulate the state must keep the prison on average ninety percent full or pay fees to make up the difference. By sentencing defendants to the maximum, Bidwell was not only lining his own pocket but also helping the state meet its contract quotas." The newscaster took on a concerned look. "The social issue that arises is whether private prison systems lead to longer-than-necessary sentences. We'll look into average sentences in states that have mostly for-profit prisons, such as Texas, and compare them to states like California and Oregon, which have none. So we'll have more coverage on the issue soon."

The newscaster moved on to another subject. Still stunned, Luke turned to Tara, who sat next to him. "Judge Bidwell sentenced me. He traded my life for a bribe."

"I'm so sorry. You must be devastated."

"Death is too good for him."

"I wonder how they caught him." Cree muted the TV and

came over.

"It was probably the IRS." Luke pushed off the couch, hoping no one tried to hug him. "I need to be alone." He started for his room, then changed his mind and went out for a walk. Somehow, news of the judge's corruption changed everything.

Chapter 24

Dallas watched Luke leave, wondering if she'd have another chance to pry him for intel before the takedown on Friday. He'd seemed stunned by the news of Bidwell's corruption, but Luke's comment that death was too good for the judge had almost sounded like regret. Did he wish he hadn't killed Bidwell, so the judge could spend the rest of his life in prison and get to experience it for himself? That would have been better karma, if you believed in that kind of thing.

"Ready for that chess game now?" Cree plopped on the couch beside her.

"Sure, but you're probably out of my league."

"Because I'm a techie? Not all coders are good strategists." He laughed again, a mellow sound she'd come to enjoy. "But I'm better than average. Let's play. I need to get my mind off all this heavy shit." Cree reached for a small coffee table, pushed the magazines off it, and yanked it toward them. A chessboard was embedded in the surface. Cree opened a drawer and pulled out a set of carved wooden pieces.

"Nice," Dallas said, touching the wood. "Is this yours?"

"I bought it at a local garage sale after we moved here."

"Sweet deal." She started setting up the pieces. "I call black."

"I knew you would. I like to think of myself as a white hat anyway."

She recognized the hacker term for those who used their skills in a positive way. "You do have the right motives."

"My family doesn't think so."

"Families never do." She moved a pawn just to get the game rolling. "I hope there's more tequila in the kitchen. Are you up for shots?"

"I have something better." Cree pulled a small mint-candy container from the drawer and removed a joint. "You toke?" He lit up before she could answer.

A pungent aroma she hadn't experienced in years. "No, it just makes me sleepy." Dallas stood. "But I do need another beer."

She brought the tequila too, just in case Luke came back and wanted to drink with her. Or Cree changed his mind. Getting people drunk had proved successful in learning their secrets. She could drink like a sailor and puke on cue to stay more sober than her target. Dallas settled into the couch again, a little closer to Cree. Physical proximity was effective too. "How did you get connected to Luke and the inner circle?"

"We met at a skydive a few years ago." He took another drag of the joint.

"I remember now. We talked about it that first night we all hung out. I guess I'm curious about why you're willing to take such risks for this cause. Considering your background."

Cree gave her a wounded look. "That's why I'm willing. I don't want to be just another spoiled rich kid. I want my life to mean something."

Dallas patted his leg. "I'm sorry. I didn't mean to be offensive. That's why I joined too. I was just drifting before.

It's important to have purpose."

Cree made a standard move, giving no hint of his chess strategy.

"What was your first mission with the group?" Dallas asked.

"A phony email campaign, supposedly sent by Congressman Bletzo to his constituents. Luke wrote the text, but I hacked his account and orchestrated the digital part." Cree smiled with pride.

A piece of information she hadn't known. "Was it effective?"

"We think so. Two weeks later, his state voted to legalize medical pot." Cree took another hit from his joint. "A small victory, but that's how we started, working to change drug laws."

Dallas studied the board and moved her rook. Cree was either not that good at the game or was about to blow her away. "What's next for the inner circle? Especially now that funding is a problem?"

"I don't know." He stiffened a little. "I'm worried about Abby. She's becoming radicalized, and I'm afraid she'll push Luke to do something regrettable, maybe even violent."

An opening. "Is Luke capable of violence?"

"I don't see him that way." Cree's voice dropped to almost a whisper. "But Luke told me once that everyone who spends that long in prison starts to see violence as just another behavior, almost a way of communicating."

Dallas repressed a shiver. Considering the millions of people incarcerated, most of whom would be free someday, that was a lot of potential trouble. She made another move on the board, eager to be alone so she could leave the house and contact Drager. She would have to go for a long walk again to get out of the range of Aaron's monitoring before she made the call.

Cree beat her in three more moves and was very gracious about it. Dallas excused herself. "I think I'm going out for some fresh air too. After I get my jacket." She hurried upstairs. Contacting her team would be so much simpler if she could just use email. Dallas pulled on her running jacket, grabbed her cell phone, and headed back down. Outside, the air had cooled but the night was clear, and above her hundreds of stars sparkled, something she never saw in Phoenix or DC, where the city lights drowned out the night sky. Dallas started down the gravel driveway to the main road.

She hoped to run into Luke and offer him comfort. He seemed vulnerable at the moment and might reveal something important. The bureau needed to know more about their plans to sabotage prison supply trucks—in case the mission or the takedown didn't go as planned Friday. Luke had been reluctant to talk about the subject.

At the road, she went left and jogged past the field to a turnout where it was safer to stand. She didn't expect much traffic, but outside this little pocket of rural hideaway, the whole area was densely populated, at least compared to large chunks of land in the southwest and Midwest. Dallas pulled out her cell phone and punched in Drager's number. Then she hesitated. Calling her contact from the Tara phone was still a risk. Aaron might be able to access her data once she was back in range. She'd only called Drager once last Sunday, but she'd been much farther away from the house. Cree and Aaron both had mad tech skills, and sometimes people like that spied on others just for fun. But Drager needed to know they were set for Friday. She remembered Drager's backup plan to comment on the Real Food blog. That seemed safer.

Dallas deleted the number and jogged back toward the house. As she approached the driveway, headlights appeared. Someone was leaving the farmhouse. The van barely stopped before it entered the road with Abby driving. What was she doing? It seemed late to be making another trip into town. Was she buying more meth to try again with the governor? Dallas was glad this case would be over Friday. She didn't want to face another ordeal like that again. She slowed to a walk down the driveway but didn't see Luke anywhere.

The common areas of the house were empty, and she hustled upstairs without running into anyone. This assignment was so different from the last two she'd done. It had taken a lot longer to get inside her target group this time, but once she'd been accepted, she'd had a lot more direct involvement with their activities, so there had been less need for spying. Her testimony—plus Luke's downloaded files— might be all the bureau needed to prosecute the inner circle for sabotage and vandalism. But the cyber crimes would be harder to prove. Drager knew that and wanted a big bust and long sentences. The irony of it was almost painful. Thinking about Luke in prison for twenty years made her stomach clench. Unless he had killed the judge. But if Bidwell had sold hundreds of people to an undeserving life of incarceration, his death didn't need any justice. This case was fucked up and she wanted out. Cameron was in Arizona, pining for her. She couldn't wait to get home and screw his brains out.

Up in her room, Dallas retrieved her laptop from between the mattresses and logged into the Real Food website. The newest blog was about fasting for short periods and how to do it safely. Dallas skimmed the article for something to respond to and scrolled down to the Comments section. It would be challenging to use Drager's code words, plus weave in the day and time of the sting, while trying to post something intelligent. After a minute of thinking, she logged in and wrote: *I'm sure humans fasted for periods of time as hunter/gatherers, but not eating on certain days seems silly. Like Catholics not eating meat on Friday. What's that about? It's just one of many peculiar human food issues. When you go to the religious texts, the inconsistencies make the directives about when not to eat certain foods meaningless. It's better to target a daily caloric intake and eat whatever real food pleases you.*

Good enough. *Hunter, Friday, one, go* and *target* should give Drager everything he needed. He probably wouldn't see the comment tonight, but he still had plenty of time to set up. She clicked Post and switched over to watch dance videos on YouTube. She'd give Drager an hour to respond, then check again in the morning. Her phone made a funny beep, and she looked over at it. Time to update her settings. She plugged the cell into her computer and went to brush her teeth. Thirty-six more hours and it would be over.

Chapter 25

Thursday, Oct. 9, 6:17 a.m.

Drager woke with a throbbing pain in his left eye. He rubbed it for a minute before getting up. A morning ritual now. The medication he took for the tumor wasn't working any more, and the surgery was risky. He was putting it off until the bureau forced him to retire at age fifty-seven. Jocelyn had pushed for the surgery, and that issue had become another wedge between them. She'd also nagged him to eat healthier and take the statins his doctor prescribed. God, he missed her.

He took a twenty-minute walk just so he could tell her he'd started exercising, then ate a banana and some beef jerky for breakfast. That was healthy, right? He couldn't stop thinking about Joce. Would he see her again on the Bidwell case? If not, he would call and ask her to lunch. He could use their son Kyle as an excuse. Drager strapped on his service weapon, grabbed his briefcase, and headed out of his new condo rental. He was closer to work now that they'd separated, but he hating living alone. Jocelyn hadn't put their house on the market yet, so maybe she was subconsciously waiting, hoping he would come back. He realized now he wanted that more than anything.

He bought a tall cup of decaf at the coffee shop near the field office and hurried through the security process. His eye ached, and he was still hungry, but he felt more upbeat than he had in months. At his desk, Drager sipped his still-too-hot coffee and called the Virginia Power Cooperative. The utility company serviced the farmhouse where the inner circle was based. A customer-service rep asked how she could help him. "Agent Drager, FBI. I need to talk to your supervisor." He knew better than to waste time with people who didn't know anything or weren't authorized to share what they did know.

Another woman, older and more assertive, came on the line. "This is Angela Milton. How can I help you?"

Drager introduced himself again, giving his badge number this time. "I need to know if Luke Maddox pays the bill at 1577 Wolf Run Road. He's wanted for murder, and we're trying to find him." The request was a long shot, and the manager would probably protect her customer.

"Oh my. Let me get back to you." She put him on hold with country music playing. Drager muted his phone.

A judge had finally signed the subpoena to check Luke Maddox's credit card and phone records for the window time surrounding Bidwell's murder, but it turned out the activist didn't have any services in his name. No financial accounts, no cell phone service, no rental agreements. A dead end. Based on Dallas' intel report of Wolf Run and "the seventh driveway past Butt's Corner," Drager had been able to pinpoint the house and its address. The owner turned out to be a real estate company with an address in Japan. So far, he'd learned nothing about the connection between the company and the inner circle, and no money exchange had surfaced. Maddox was careful about hiding his tracks.

The utility manager came back on line. "The account is

held by Hana Kasumi. She's had service at the address for eighteen years."

Another dead end. Or maybe not. "How is the bill paid?"

"It's on autopay with a credit card."

"Will you give me the number?"

"I can't do that. Not without a court order."

"I'll get one. What's your fax number?"

Drager noted it on his yellow tablet—a disposable piece of information. He'd learned to categorize, so the paper pileup in his office didn't overwhelm him. By the time he got the subpoena for the utility payment number and waited for the credit card company to send him records, it would be next week. He sent a quick email to Chuck Surry, in the White Collar unit: *How are you coming on the bank accounts for the inner circle?* Surry, who had contacts in the financial world, was checking into Abby Gleeson and Cree Songchild—plus his real name of Drake Morrison— to see if they had bank accounts or credit cards.

Maybe it was time to check the Real Food blog again to see if Dallas had posted anything. UC agents were often lax about checking in, but in this case, Dallas was being monitored by her targets, and it made him nervous to not hear from her. He opened the blog from a bookmark and scrolled through the comments. There she was. Tara Adams had posted a rambling comment about food choices, but he read the message loud and clear. The inner circle would be at Senator Pearlman's home on Friday at one, so he could get his people in place for a takedown. *Excellent!* That was fast. Agent Dallas had a reputation for speed and manipulation, and he was impressed. The activists had also been ripe for stepping up their game. But this was happening almost too fast. He had to call Senator Pearlman and prep him and his wife for Friday, then get out to their house and map the layout. Plus pull in more agents for the operation.

Before he could do any of that, two emails landed at the same time. The first was from the Agent Surry: *Songchild has a credit card that is paid automatically by an account connected to the American Tradition Foundation, a private charity. But no large transfers of cash. Sorry.* That was disappointing. Where and how did the inner circle access their money? Drager was impatient to find the source.

The second email was from the manager at the Grand Roosevelt Hotel, and it had an attachment: *This file was recorded by one of the guests at the fundraiser for Senator Pearlman. It has the voiceover the activists used. Can you compare it to known criminals?*

Drager smiled to himself. Yes, the bureau had recordings of some criminals, and now banks were capturing thousands more of potential criminals. But the issue wasn't about identifying the perps—they knew who they were. It was a matter of collecting all the evidence they could to convict them. The recording would help. He wondered which one of the inner circle had made it. They would know soon enough.

Agent Wunn stepped into his workspace. Open doors were the policy in this field office.

"I found something that could be important." Her typically expressionless face held a tremor of nervousness.

"What have you got?"

"I've been running the activists' names into every database I could think of, hoping to find other aliases they might have used." She paused and sat down. "There's an Aaron Foster in the witness protection program."

Chapter 26

Thursday, Oct. 9, 10:49 a.m.

Luke pulled off his sweaty biking clothes and stood in a hot shower. He'd ridden twenty-five miles, trying to burn up the stress, his brain racing as fast as his legs. He couldn't stop thinking about the mission tomorrow. The decriminalization vote was critical, and none of the other efforts they'd tried with Pearlman had worked. The senator's announcement, claiming that the more he was targeted, the more intractable he would become, had infuriated him. So the dog-napping/blackmail tactic was critical to finally getting some forward momentum. The mission seemed simple to execute, and Luke wanted to be optimistic. Cree was out there in the senator's neighborhood now, watching the house to see if they'd beefed up security. Cree had texted earlier to report no sign of anything new and would be on his way home soon. Everything indicated a green light for the mission. Yet, uneasiness plagued Luke.

Luke stepped out of the shower and dried off, trying to put his finger on exactly what seemed wrong. Abby, for starters. She'd been tense and irritable at times and fiercely upbeat at others. Their breakup could be to blame, but the headspace she was in at the moment made him wonder if he could trust her in a tight situation. He would feel better about the mission if she stayed home. They didn't need everyone to be there. But he knew Abby would freak out if he suggested it, and he didn't have the patience to argue with her.

As he pulled on jeans, his thoughts came back to Judge Bidwell. He'd always assumed the mean bastard had sentenced him to ten years out of a sincere belief that drugs were evil and people who did drugs needed to be locked up. As hard as that was to accept, at least it was an honest sociopolitical difference of perspective. But to know the judge had done it for profit filled Luke with such rage and despair he felt almost dysfunctional. If someone hadn't already killed the judge, Luke would happily do it himself for the peace of mind. Or so he thought. But now he couldn't even confront the man. How could he process his rage and move forward? He had to find a way to accept this new reality about his lost years.

A loud knock jarred him. Before he could answer, Abby burst in. "Hey, you're looking good." She closed and locked the door behind her.

Luke reached for a T-shirt shirt off the bed. Abby needed to stop thinking about him in a sexual way.

She rushed at him and grabbed the shirt. "Don't get dressed. I like your naked chest." She moved in and rubbed his nipples.

Luke grabbed her hands and stepped back. "Please don't. That part of our relationship is over."

"Oh come on. I'm not asking to be your girlfriend again. Just your fuck buddy." She grinned, her eyes dancing with lust.

"I'm sorry, but it's best if we keep it simple, everyone in the house on equal terms." He'd been careful to avoid alone time with Tara too, so Abby wouldn't be jealous and spiteful.

He hadn't expected her to take it as sign that he was still available.

Abby scoffed. "There is no true equality, ever. Even utopian societies never achieve it."

He didn't have the heart for a philosophical discussion. "Unless we have business to discuss, I think you should leave."

"We do have business." She let go of the T-shirt and plopped down in his desk chair.

Luke pulled on the shirt and sat on the bed. "What is it?"

"Why aren't we following through with Aaron's idea of interrupting prison supply trucks?"

They'd had this conversation. "Because it's dangerous and doesn't accomplish much. To be effective, we would have to do it on a much bigger scale, and when you start involving that many people, things get sloppy."

She slammed her hand on the desk. "You're too cautious, and we're getting nowhere."

Luke clenched his hands and counted to three. "We're making a big play tomorrow, and it will produce long-term results. This is a lifetime commitment. Civil rights take decades to win."

"I don't have decades," Abby whined. "I have Hep C and colitis, and I won't live to be forty. I want to feel good about what we've accomplished before I'm too sick to give a shit."

He often forgot about her illnesses because she rarely brought them up. He'd been fortunate to get out of prison after a decade with only emotional scars. He'd had staph infection and food poisoning while incarcerated, but neither carried long-term effects. Most ex-cons weren't that lucky. Stress could ruin the immune system, and prisons were rampant with contagious diseases like hepatitis and tuberculosis.

Luke softened his voice to show compassion. "You *will* see progress, I promise. And you may get treatment for the Hep C someday. There's some new drugs out there."

"But not for Medicaid patients."

They'd had this conversation too. He suspected she was just feeling lonely, maybe a little depressed. But he had too many other things on his mind. "Eventually, those meds will be available to everyone." Luke stood, walked to the door, and opened it. "I still have more preparation for our mission tomorrow. Will you give me some space?"

She laughed. "You worry too much. Tomorrow will be easier than the damn fundraisers we've targeted. We'll be alone in the house with lookouts on either end of the street."

Her cavalier attitude reinforced his concerns. "Anything can happen, and if you don't realize that, maybe you should excuse yourself tomorrow."

Abby blinked and her mouth dropped open. "Are you telling me to stay home?" She raised her voice. "You think I'm a risk?"

"Carelessness is always a risk."

"Fuck you. I'll be fine." She stormed out, shaking her head.

Luke breathed a sigh of relief. He sat down at his computer and opened a Google Earth image of the senator's house. His cell phone rang, and he jumped a little. Boy, he was wound tight. Luke glanced at the ID: Jason. One of the only JRN members who knew how to contact him directly. Jason was a friend, but he didn't officially know about the inner circle's activities. Luke pressed the speaker button and answered the call.

"It's Jason. Are you sitting down?"

Dread settled into his stomach. He opened his sock drawer, took out the anti-anxiety medication he'd bought online, and dissolved one under his tongue. He rarely took it, but sometimes he had PTSD prison nightmares he couldn't shake. "I'm ready. What is it?"

"Judge Bidwell is dead. Murdered. He handled your case, right?"

His shoulders relaxed. "Yes, and I heard about the bribes too."

Jason cleared his throat. "Did you see the breaking news? About the court clerk?"

The panic was back. "No. What?"

"Callie Sayers, who clerked for Bidwell for ten years, was murdered too."

It took him a moment to process the full implications. "How and when did she die?" Maybe it had been a random coincidence.

"She was shot in the face sometime last week and dumped at a construction site."

"Holy hell." Luke turned back to his computer and googled her name to see if a news report would come up. Several did, and he started scanning, but the information was limited. Still, it was clear Callie Sayers had died before the judge. Had Bidwell killed her to keep her quiet? The evil motherfucker!

Jason made a nervous sound in his throat. "I'll bet the police are looking for you."

Another punch in the gut. He hadn't considered that. Would the cops try to frame him for the murder? Maybe he had to rethink everything.

Chapter 27

Thursday, Oct. 9, 1:30 p.m.

Jocelyn read the ballistic section of the forensic report and caught herself grinding her teeth. She reached for some gum—she refused to wear the damn mouth guard during the day. She'd already heard from the ME that the gun was fired at close range, six feet or less, and that both bullets had exited the victim. Even if she found the killer and he still had possession of the weapon, without bullets or casings to compare grooves, it wouldn't mean much. She stood to stretch, wishing she had an adjustable desk that would let her stand up at work. She'd asked for one, but the department had balked at the eight hundred dollars, saying she needed a doctor's note. And she had no intention of seeing a doctor.

After a minute, she sat back down and called the victim's cell phone carrier again. She needed the damn phone records to see who Callie had interacted with the day of her death. The killer had obviously disposed of her purse, phone, and shoes. Jocelyn suspected the victim had been tortured and shot in her car, and the bullets were embedded in the seatback. The vehicle, along with all her personal items, had probably been dumped into the river or dropped off at a crushing operation. She would have her partner look into that too.

Jocelyn had already contacted the organizers of the veteran's event Callie had come to DC to attend. Her car wasn't in their parking lot, and they had no way of knowing if she'd ever been there. This case was maddening. The perp was clearly someone who knew how to cover up a crime. Judge Bidwell was a prime suspect, but she couldn't exactly bring him in for questioning. But she could look at his phone and credit card records to see where he'd been on Tuesday.

Knowing that her most likely suspect was dead had taken some of the time pressure off the investigation though. Now it was a matter of following up every lead and digging up all the little pieces of evidence to make a solid case. If she was right about Judge Bidwell, they would never go to court, but Callie's family deserved closure, and the people of Virginia needed to know the whole truth. Jocelyn took a long drink of soda and opened a digital subpoena form.

"What are you working on?" Sergeant Murphy's voice boomed behind her.

She turned and tried not to appear rattled. "A subpoena for Judge Bidwell's phone records."

"We have those, and I'll get you a copy."

Of course. The rest of the team was working to solve the judge's murder. What a bizarre turn of events.

Murphy raised an eyebrow. "Anyone from the Justice department call you?"

"Not yet. Maybe now that Bidwell is dead, they closed out the charges against him and moved on. Callie Sayers may not be important to them."

The sergeant brought his hands to his hips. "She ended up in our jurisdiction, so we will resolve this, even if her killer has already received his own brand of justice."

That sounded like she would get some help with it.

"Thanks. Anything new on the judge's case?" Ross would want to know, and she'd been thinking about calling him.

"A surveillance camera caught someone leaving the parking garage on foot, but not the perp's face. Slender, five-eight or nine, and dressed in all black." The sergeant scowled. "Luke Maddox, your ex-husband's favorite suspect, is that height, but when he left prison, he was two hundred pounds. So unless he's lost a lot of weight, it wasn't him."

"The person leaving on foot might not be the killer either. The perp may have driven in and out." She wasn't defending Ross, just pointing out the obvious.

"We've looked at all the vehicle footage from the garage, and none of the license plates are connected to the judge or belong to any ex-cons that are connected to him." Murphy still loomed over her.

Jocelyn stood to straighten her back and be at his level. "Has the team tracked the judge's whereabouts for Tuesday evening?" She'd called Murphy on the drive home the day before to update him, so he knew Bidwell was a viable suspect in the clerk's murder.

"His wife says he told her he went out to see a movie, but she thinks he was seeing another woman."

An idea hit her. "Or a prostitute. My victim had a hooker's ID. I haven't found her yet, but she might know something about the judge."

"Keep me posted."

As soon as the sergeant walked away, her partner came into her workspace. John Snyder was chubby, pale as a ghost, and had no lips to speak of. When she'd first started working with him, she'd found him hard to look at, but now it didn't matter.

"It's about damn time." She gave a half smile. "I'm glad

you're feeling better."

"Me too. That was the worst case of flu I've ever had." He grabbed the visitor's chair and sat down. "I'm sorry I haven't been here. But I've read your reports, and I feel like I'm up to speed. What can I do first?"

It was only fair to give him the grunt work. "Find a prostitute named Sherry Jones. I'd start with her cousin, Kaylin Parshelle. I've already been to Jones' last known address, and it's a dead end."

Snyder's smooth forehead crinkled. "Are you sure that's a good use of my time?"

"The hooker's ID was on the victim, so maybe she knows the killer."

"I get it. What else?"

"Check out local junkyards and see if the victim's car was brought in for crushing, then help me peruse her bank and phone records when they come in. We're behind on this one because of the wrong ID."

Snyder blinked and scrunched up his face. A moment later, he grabbed his stomach and convulsed. "I have to go." He spun and ran toward the hall, presumably heading to the restroom. Apparently, he wasn't over being sick. Jocelyn downed the rest of her soda and turned back to her computer screen. This would be another long day.

Her email notification lit up, and she opened the new message. It was a brief note from an administrator at the cell phone service provider, apologizing for the delay, but her message included a PDF attachment. *Yes!* Jocelyn opened the document and scanned down, looking for last Tuesday. Eventually, she would note every call in the weeks before, but right now she needed to know who Callie Sayers had talked to on the day she was murdered.

Only three calls on Tuesday. Jocelyn plugged the first number into the dispatcher's database and came up with Rona Jeffers. A quick Facebook search revealed her to be a twenty-something woman who lived in Richmond. Probably just a friend Callie had called. She added her to the case notes and keyed in the next number, an incoming call. It belonged to Eastern National. *Interesting.* The victim hadn't banked there, but the business seemed familiar. She'd seen or heard it recently, most likely associated with the judge's death. Jocelyn skimmed her team's printed case notes for Judge Bidwell. She didn't find the bank at first and had to read through again more slowly. But there it was near the end. The widow, Joan Bidwell, was a president of Eastern National.

Why had she called Callie Sayers three hours before her murder?

Chapter 28

Thursday, Oct. 9, 2:37 p.m.

Aaron Mortlock opened a beer and eased into his recliner with his laptop. He was sick of staying in this small funky room in the middle of nowhere, putting up with a bunch of loser activists. A dying man deserved better—such as a penthouse in a Las Vegas hotel surrounded by strippers—but after tomorrow, his brother would be free and he could move on. For now, he continued his search of Tara's computer. He clicked a random file and scrolled through it, a Word manuscript that looked like an autobiography. He'd accessed her hard drive remotely when she first joined the group, so he could monitor her activities for a while, just as a precaution. The search he'd done at the time had been superficial. Other people's photos and recipes bored him. But now he needed to know everything.

Tara's post the night before on the Real Food Blog had been strange. Her browser history revealed that she'd visited the site twice in the last week, but never before, which seemed odd. But she had bothered him from the beginning. Tara was too pretty under the heavy makeup, too healthy, and too normal to be an activist or an ex-con. And for him, she seemed to come out of nowhere. The others had met her months ago at a skydive, and she'd moved to DC shortly after.

He knew enough about how the feds operated to smell a rat when they came around.

So far, he hadn't found any evidence she was in contact with the FBI. Unless that post had been a coded warning. He opened the Real Food blog again and scrolled through the comments. Another visitor had responded to Tara's post, a brief supportive *I agree.* Aaron scrolled back through other blogs on the site. The responder, *luckyjones*, had never commented before. Was it an exchange of information or was he just being paranoid? Tara had gone out for a walk the night before too. Had she made a phone call? He searched her Wi-Fi update history and found the link to her phone. No recent calls. The last one had been made on Monday morning. That was when she'd driven him to the clinic. Was it another coincidence that the only call she'd made had been while she was out of monitoring range? Now that he had the number, he could find out who it belonged to.

After twenty-five minutes of hacking wireless carrier databases—or more accurately, re-entering because he'd been inside of all them before—he had the service account. But no name was associated with it. A cash account on a cheap burner phone. Who owned those except criminals and people with something to hide? He had a couple himself.

On top of all that, Tara didn't have enough files to be a writer, unless she was really new at it. She also didn't seem to exist before last year, not in an in-depth way. He had to conclude that Tara Adams was an alias. No, a bullshit background constructed by the feds. She was an undercover agent, sent to take them all down. Only there was no *all*. He didn't care about justice reform—except to get his brother out of prison. Which was happening tomorrow.

A panicked thought rattled his heart. The feds could be

on their way right now. If they came to the farmhouse, he would take Tara hostage and use her as a shield. One option was to pack up his meager belongings and get the hell out now. But he had to deal with Tara, or whatever her name was, either way. If he left her alive, she would be suspicious of his sudden departure and come after him—or send other agents to intercept him. He couldn't let them take him, not now that he was so close to pulling this off. The transfer he'd been working toward, using bribes and extortion, was finally happening.

Aaron stood and went to the window, hoping to be inspired. But he was tired of looking at alfalfa fields and oak groves. This had been a long four months, and his only pleasure had been shafting politicians who thought tough prison sentences were good for society. He'd also learned a lot about hacking from Cree. That had been a huge bonus. He'd joined the group with the sole purpose of using them to help free Shawn. Plus he'd needed a place to hide for a while.

What the hell would he do about Tara? She posed the biggest threat to Luke and the others, who were probably walking into an FBI sting at the senator's house tomorrow. He could tell them about Tara, but not one of them had the balls to kill her, the only sure way to protect themselves. He could shoot her without qualm, but he didn't have the strength to get rid of her body. Letting the others get busted and go to prison would be the best way to protect himself. He had a little longer to live than he'd led them to believe. Not much, but he had no intention of spending it in a courtroom or jail cell.

His brother, though, still had a full life, and Aaron had promised his mother he'd get Shawn out, one way or another. Tomorrow, Shawn would be transferred from a high-security federal prison in Lee County to a medium-security prison across the river seventy miles away. During the trip, the van would pass along a narrow stretch of road that curved between canyon walls, creating an area of low visibility from a distance. And just beyond that was a gravel turnout where he would be waiting, a frail man, lying in the road, his disabled car nearby. When the guard got close enough, Aaron would shoot him, then show the bomb to the driver before he could react.

No, that was too risky. He had to stab the guard and use him as a shield when he approached the van. Once the armed driver could see the bomb, Aaron could force him to release his prisoner. Or he could set off the bomb as the van approached, forcing it off the road, then shoot the driver. But that would put Shawn at risk. Aaron had been over this in his mind a few times, but none of the strategies were ideal. This would go smoother if he'd been able to enlist the inner circle's help. But he'd failed to persuade Luke that sabotaging prison supply trucks was useful to their cause. He needed someone else to bear the risk of the bomb.

He heard Tara's door open and close.

Someone expendable, like the federal agent who needed to die.

Aaron moved to his own door, opened it a crack, and watched her jog down the stairs in workout clothes. She was going out for a run. An idea popped into his head. A way to solve both problems in the same clever plan. But he had to move fast to get her under control. He stepped into the hall and shuffled quickly to her door. Luke and Abby had rooms downstairs, so they weren't likely to be around, but Cree was more unpredictable. Aaron twisted the knob and stepped in. The house was old, and none of the bedroom doors originally had keyed entries. He'd added a lock to his own when he first moved in, but he had plenty to hide from the others. Tara hadn't even been allowed to bring her car out yet, so she hadn't had the opportunity to make herself comfortable in her crappy little room. But she hadn't complained about it because she didn't plan to stay long.

Aaron went straight to her bed and lifted the mattress. A silver laptop was tucked in the middle. Why was she hiding it? He'd found nothing incriminating in her files, but he'd expected to find a service weapon. Had she come into this assignment without a gun? Too bad for her. Aaron started with her dresser, searching every drawer and shoving his hand into every pocket and sock. But she hadn't brought much clothing out to the house. He moved to the small private half bath and snooped through her medicine cabinet and makeup bag. Inside a tiny metal Carmex container, he found three blue-and-white capsules. *Well, well.* He suspected they were some kind of sedative. Perfect. Aaron pocketed the pills and kept searching everything. The only other item of interest was the switchblade he found in her backpack. He looked around, plotting how to set up the whole thing. He needed Tara unconscious, but it would be best to lure her into his room first, where he could strap the explosive on her behind a locked door. Then he would keep her from communicating with anyone.

A half-empty bottle of green Gatorade sat on her desk. That would do nicely. She would drink it all down after her run, then get sleepy in the shower and pass out twenty or thirty minutes later, depending on what the drugs were and what dose they contained. He just had to get her into his room while she was still upright. It shouldn't be a problem. She'd already shown him affection and sympathy. His health issues were real, but the story he'd told about his sister wasn't. Actually, it was true, it was just someone else's sister. The funeral he'd attended last week had been for his older brother, so his mother had pressured him again to get Shawn, her youngest, out of prison.

Aaron opened Tara's laptop, googled a description of the meds, and quickly confirmed they were flunitrazipam, otherwise known as Rohypnol, or roofies. Who had the spy-bitch planned to use these on? Aaron opened the Gatorade bottle and pulled one of the capsules out of his pocket. When he held it over the small opening, his left hand trembled. *Shit.* Why now? He waited a moment, took a breath, and broke open the pill. The white powder tumbled into the plastic bottle. Was that enough? The pills were probably a one-milligram dose, enough to reduce anxiety, but not enough to knock her out. He opened another capsule over the bottleneck, but his hand shook, and he spilled some of it down the side and on the desk. *Oh fucking hell.* The damn tremors had started a month ago, and he didn't know why. Maybe it was the medication he was taking for the pulmonary fibrosis.

How much of the sedative had he lost? Should he dump in the final pill too? No, another full dose might knock her out too soon, and he didn't want her passed out in her own bedroom. That could ruin the whole plan.

Aaron shoved the empty gel casings back into his pocket, put the lid on the Gatorade, and shook the bottle. The lime-colored liquid had a slight cloudy look. Not good. Would it dissipate in time? Would she even notice? He grabbed the bottle and hurried to the bathroom to rinse off the spilled powder, then used wet toilet paper to clean up the mess on the desk. He flushed the toilet paper, put the Gatorade carefully back in the exact spot he'd found it, and glanced around. Had he moved anything else? Her laptop! He grabbed it off the bed and shoved it under the mattress, hoping he'd hit the right place.

Aaron listened at the door for a moment. No movement in the hall or on the stairs. He slipped out of Tara's room and hurried back to his own space. She might return at any moment. He was ready.

Thursday, Oct. 9, 3:33 p.m.

Dallas sprinted for the driveway, finally ready to stop. She'd pushed herself to run farther than usual. The week at the farmhouse with little to do—interrupted only by a long sit in jail and court—had made her restless. Once she'd worked her way in, this case hadn't proved to be particularly challenging. Her targets willingly shared their criminal plans, and they'd been easy to manipulate into taking a bigger risk. Thankfully, the arrests would happen tomorrow. She might have days of debriefing and reports to fill out before she could go home, but at least she would be free in the evening to go clubbing. She couldn't wait to call Cameron and have a little phone sex.

The thought made her smile, and she slowed to a walk down the gravel lane. Another twenty-four hours as Tara Adams, justice-reform activist, and she could mentally move on. A pang of guilt tugged at her. Luke and the others would be moving to prison cells. But that wasn't her fault. They would have eventually conducted the home-invasion mission or something worse without her nudging. And if the bureau wasn't there to intercept them, an innocent person might be hurt or killed. The inner circle had admirable goals, but they were on the wrong path. Still, she couldn't wait to get away from Luke. Looking him in the eyes had become difficult.

Back at the house, she stopped for a quick gulp of water in the kitchen and headed for the stairs. No one was hanging out in the common space, and she was glad she didn't have to socialize. Luke made her feel guilty, Abby pissed her off, and Cree wasn't someone she could take seriously. Aaron intrigued her, but she didn't think he would open up to her, and his illness was sad to witness. So she hurried to her bedroom and closed the door. She'd be happy to get out of this space too. The pale green walls bugged her, and she didn't have a comfortable chair to sit in.

Peeling off her jacket, she crossed the room, then removed her shoes. She needed a shower, but she hated the one in the hall bathroom, with its narrow iron-stained walls and lukewarm water. She had more exercise to do first anyway. Dallas took a long swallow of Gatorade, then lowered herself to the area rug on the floor. After a series of crunches, she began a stretching routine. Her stomach growled, and she considered making a trip to the kitchen for something to eat. But she had noticed the cupboards and refrigerator seemed to be running low, and she wondered who did the shopping and when. Not that it mattered now. She wouldn't be here next week.

She got to her feet and downed the rest of the Gatorade. The drink would hold her until later. Might as well shower, then read on her laptop for a while to pass some time. A knocking sound surprised her. Was Abby here to threaten her again? At the door, Dallas hesitated, then asked, "Who is it?"

"Aaron. I need your help with something."

She opened the door. "What is it?"

"I dropped my medication behind the desk, and I need to move it, so I can reach the bottle. Embarrassing as this is, I don't have the strength to do it myself." He gave her a sad smile. "Damn lungs. They cut off my blood supply."

"No problem." Dallas stepped out and followed him next door. Her legs trembled, and she suddenly felt weak herself. How far had she run?

Inside Aaron's room, powerful odors assaulted her. Sweaty sheets, stale beer, and something bitter. An ache throbbed in her temples from the smell. The visual clutter was almost as bad. Did he ever throw anything away? He was sick, but that was no excuse. And what the hell was he making on that workbench?

"It's this desk," he said, shuffling across the room, kicking clothes out of the way.

Dallas froze. Something was really wrong, but she couldn't think straight. Dizziness washed over her, and her head swirled. *What the hell?* She took a deep breath to clear her mind. Big mistake. The top half of her body flopped forward, with her hands resting on her legs. What was happening ? She felt drugged. *Oh dear god.*

Panic flooded her. She *was* drugged, and Aaron had done it. But why? To rape her? She turned to run and staggered sideways into an armchair. *Get up!* She screamed in her mind, but she couldn't make herself move. Her muscles had turned to jello, and she seemed to have lost control. Dallas opened her mouth to scream for help, but her cry was so weak, it fell dead before it reached the wall. *Fuh...*

Blackness overcame her, and her brain shut down.

Chapter 30

Thursday, Oct. 9, 1:05 p.m.

Drager went out, despite the light rain, and bought a ham-and-swiss sandwich at a nearby Potbelly. He ate at his desk and washed it down with a rare glass of water, part of his new healthier program, then glanced at his desk phone again. No blinking light. He'd called WITSEC twice and left messages, but the marshals hadn't gotten back to him yet.

He turned to the stack of banking documents and picked up where he'd left off. Maddox had to have a holding company that money flowed through. Or else he used an alias to access an account. Drager was determined to uncover who had been funding the acts of sabotage, and he suspected the activists would never tell him, even after they were caught.

His phone rang and he snatched it up. "Agent Drager."

"This is Tim Arbuckle with the Marshal's Service, returning your call."

About time. "I have an undercover agent who's encountered someone named Aaron Foster. The name is in WITSEC's database, but there's no information about him."

"Let me see what I can find." The line was quiet for a minute, but he could hear chatter in the background. The marshal came back on. "You couldn't find anything because Aaron Foster, aka Aaron Mortlock, is dead."

Mortlock? Dead? Drager didn't know whether to rejoice or panic. "You mean Aaron Mortlock, the fraud ringmaster and brother of Shawn Mortlock, the domestic terrorist?"

"Yes, but Aaron died five months ago. Pulmonary fibrosis. Even bad guys get sick."

How did witness protection handle those deaths? He'd never thought about it before. "Did you contact his family?"

"We don't do that. They would still be at risk."

"Where was he living at the time?"

"Ohio."

"All right. We must be dealing with a different Aaron Foster. Thanks for the call."

"Any time." The marshal hung up.

His team had found a dozen Aaron Fosters so far, just not the right one yet. Drager tried to get back to his financial documents, but the possible connection to Aaron and Shawn Mortlock unnerved him. He opened the Real Food blog again. Nothing from Dallas. He had to assume the group was preparing for their mission, and she didn't want to risk anything by contacting him. He had to let it go. UC agents were notorious for not checking in. He posted another comment, communicating that he wanted to hear from her, then went back to reading bank statements.

At four that afternoon, Drager pulled into the driveway of Senator Pearlman's property and shut off his car. A newer building with a sleek modern design, the house stood out among all the gabled roofs and dormer windows in the rest of the upscale neighborhood. Pearlman had done well for himself as a corporate lawyer before winning his senate seat four terms ago. They had talked on the phone a couple of times already about the sting, and the Pearlmans were expecting him. Agent Wunn, who would be part of the arrest team, had parked on the next block over and would jog up and down the street, scouting locations where other agents could find cover tomorrow. Someone from the inner circle could be casing the house, and they didn't want to spook them by having a bunch of people in dark suits visit the senator and his neighborhood the day before their planned assault. Which reminded Drager to pull off his jacket before getting out of the car. *Damn*, he wished they'd had more time to set up.

On the walk to the house, exterior lights came on automatically. He found it interesting that the activists had timed their assault for broad daylight in the middle of the afternoon. He still wanted to know exactly what they had planned, but Dallas was obviously limited in what she could communicate through blog comments. So he and his team had to be prepared for anything. Seven agents, in addition to himself, were lined up for the operation, and a SWAT unit was on standby. This case had been unusual from the beginning, but having the UC embed with the activists had called for extra precaution. Now his team had to make sure they didn't shoot her in the takedown. Or let the assailants take her hostage.

The senator came out to greet him, shaking hands silently, with a nod of appreciation. Pearlman wasn't as big as he looked on TV, giving press statements. Only five-nine, but in good shape for a man with a full head of gray hair. Inside the house, the senator led him to a bright kitchen with an island counter and offered him a drink.

"No thanks. Where's your wife?"

"She's coming down." Pearlman poured himself something that smelled like scotch.

"Did you find the house plans with the layout?" Drager wanted to move this along. He still had to return to the office, make copies of the plans, and hold a tactical meeting.

"I did." Pearlman went into an office down the hall and came back with a cardboard tube. He pulled out the engineered drawings and laid them flat on the counter. "There are four points of entry," the senator said, pointing to markings on the perimeter. "Front door, access to the garage, and two sets of French doors to the back patio."

Drager studied the plans, mentally mapping where his people would be. Three agents would show up before daylight tomorrow to station themselves inside the home. The rest of the team would arrive over the morning and wait in neighbors' homes or in cars down the street. A few would be on the next block over, waiting for the signal. "Considering the mid-afternoon time, I expect a front-door approach," Drager said. "We know they have a van, so they'll probably pose as repairmen or cable installers."

A pretty woman entered the kitchen. "When is this supposed to happen?" She had thick shoulder-length blond hair, but her face had lost its smoothness and she was obviously in her sixties. She carried a small matching blond dog in her arms.

Drager smiled at her. "Tomorrow, sometime between one and three."

"Good, I won't be home." She held out her hand. "I'm Stella Pearlman."

He shook it, surprised by her statement. The activists had planned the assault for a time when no one was home? That didn't make sense. He glanced at the senator. "You'll be at the capitol building, correct?"

"I will. The legislation we talked about, to change

marijuana's classification, is scheduled for that time tomorrow. I'm sure the timing isn't a coincidence."

"I'm sure it's not." Drager rubbed his throbbing eyes. "But why come here if no one will be home?" He started to pace the kitchen, and the little dog yapped at him. He spun back. "Will the dog be home?"

Pearlman's jaw dropped, and his wife let out a little gasp. "You think they plan to kidnap or harm Tessie?" She hugged the little terrier closer to her chest.

"I'm not sure. We're acting on limited intel." Drager mulled it over. Mrs. Pearlman's absence from the house was both a blessing and a curse. It made the operation easier, because they didn't have to worry about her getting taken hostage or hurt in possible crossfire. But it also meant they couldn't charge the inner circle with a home invasion or kidnapping. A B&E at the most, depending on what happened with the dog.

"I'm not leaving Tessie," Mrs. Pearlman announced. "I know your people will be here, but I can't let her be traumatized."

Drager hesitated, choosing a careful response. "If no one is here when they arrive, it's not a home invasion, so we can only arrest them for breaking and entering, or maybe burglary if they try to take something, neither of which carries much of a sentence."

Mrs. Pearlman narrowed her eyes, trying to read him. "Then I'll stay home from my appointment. That way Tessie won't be traumatized, and you can arrest them for home invasion."

The senator snapped his head toward his wife. "That's a bad idea. You don't know what these people are capable of."

"But the FBI will be here." She turned back to Drager.

"You'll have agents in the house, right? People with guns to protect me."

"Guns!" The senator shook his head. "That's exactly why I don't want you home. You could get hurt."

"I won't. Because I'll know exactly what's happening." She stroked her husband's arm. "Ray, we have to put this group away for a long time. They've been targeting you for six months. They also stole your campaign funds, and you're down in the polls."

"But the bureau will be here to arrest them, with or without you." The senator's argument lacked his earlier conviction.

Drager stepped in. "She's right. On a simple B&E, some of them could be released in a year or less. Then they can start right up again. And so far, we can't prove they took your money."

Pearlman locked eyes with him. "Promise me Stella will be safe."

"She'll be fine. As far as we know, the inner circle doesn't carry guns."

"All right. What else do we need to know?"

They talked for another fifteen minutes, then Drager walked through the house, just to see the details that didn't show up on the plans. The Pearlmans invited him to stay for dinner, but he declined and left, feeling better about the whole operation. Still, it wasn't ideal. At this point, he was more worried about Dallas than Mrs. Pearlman. Why hadn't his UC found a way to contact him?

Out in the car, his phone rang, and he looked at the screen: *Jocelyn Larson, MDP.* Would this call from his ex-wife be personal or somehow related to the judge's murder? He knew the answer, but he drummed up a pleasant tone. "Hello,

Joce. What's going on?"

"You didn't make the Bidwell task force meeting."

Did she sound worried? "I know. I've got a special-op going down soon, and I'm preoccupied."

"I thought you should know Judge Bidwell's ex-clerk was murdered the day before he was."

What? The intel startled and confused him, and he made her walk him through it. "Someone who used to work for the judge was murdered?"

"Yes, Callie Sayers. She was his clerk for ten years in Richmond, Virginia."

"And she was killed a day before he died? How?"

"Shot twice in the face and dumped at a construction site in DC. With a prostitute's ID."

Bizarre. "Any leads?" He knew the answer to that.

"Just the judge. He could have killed her to keep her from testifying against him."

Drager started the car and backed into the street, while processing the possibilities. "Then Maddox could have killed the judge after he learned about the payoffs to CSA?"

"Maybe." His ex chewed something crunchy as she talked. Dinner in the car, he guessed. She continued, "Or the same person could have killed both of them. Someone else who didn't want the truth about the payoffs to come out."

He didn't want to let Luke Maddox off the hook, but the other murder changed the scenario. "Maybe it was another judge who was taking bribes too."

"I plan to look into it, but I've had a full day. You should know that someone burned her feet with a cigarette and tossed her house looking for something. My guess is evidence of the judge's crime."

Good grief. Maybe Maddox hadn't done it. He hoped

Jocelyn and her team would untangle the threads and bring someone to justice.

"Ross? Did I lose you?"

"No, I'm just getting on the road. I have to go back to the office and hold a tactical meeting, but thanks for the update." The clerk's death was intriguing, but not likely related to his case against the inner circle, especially if Luke Maddox wasn't the killer. Drager started to ask if she wanted to have dinner sometime, but Jocelyn said goodbye and hung up.

Chapter 31

Friday, Oct. 10, 9:15 a.m.

Dallas woke with a headache, and her mouth was so dry her tongue felt swollen. It took a moment to get her eyes open, and when she did, her stomach heaved. The sight of Aaron's filthy room in daylight brought it all back. The bastard had drugged her and she'd been unconscious all night. Dallas tried to get up, but couldn't move. A double strip of duct tape across her mouth kept her from swearing out loud. Her wrists were taped to the chair as well. *What the fuck?* She remembered thinking he might rape her, but this seemed worse. Where was he?

She spotted Aaron on the bed, lying down. She hoped he was asleep. With time, she could pull free. Duct tape didn't stick well to leather, and now that the drug was out of her system, she could kick his ass if he woke up. Dallas jerked up with her arms, but the tape didn't budge.

Aaron sat up. "Oh good, you're awake. We don't have much time left."

Time for what? But she couldn't ask.

He walked over, his breath ragged and foul. "I'll take the tape off your mouth as soon as we have an understanding."

Who the fuck was he? She wanted to kill him! But she needed answers too.

He pulled up his desk chair and sat in front of her, but out of range of her feet. "You have an explosive device strapped to your stomach—"

No! She sucked in her breath and looked down.

"So forget any idea of calling for help, assaulting me, or rescuing yourself."

He'd put her running jacket back on her but left it unzipped, and underneath she could see a bulge. Only about five inches long and maybe three inches deep. *Was it real? What did he want?* The pounding in her head escalated.

"You'd like to know all about it, wouldn't you?" His laughter gave way to coughing. Aaron finally got up and drank some water. Dallas desperately wanted some too, but she couldn't risk consuming more sedative.

"I'm proud of my skills, so I can't resist telling you." Aaron sat back down and leaned forward like an eager teacher. "The device has two parts. One is a glycol-based liquid, which acts as the detonator. It's powerful enough to kill you by itself. The second explosive is PETN, which is stable until it's triggered, but then, BOOM!" He gestured with both hands, indicating it could take down the house.

Aaron reached behind him and pulled out a big silver gun. *A Glock.* He smiled, his small teeth making him look like a nasty rodent. "I can also shoot you in the head without triggering the glycol."

Dallas swallowed to wet her throat.

"I'll take the tape off your mouth if you're ready to shut up and listen."

Dallas nodded. She had to be able to talk to him, find out what she could. He ripped the piece off her mouth in a quick painful movement.

She swallowed again, and her lips felt cracked. "Who are

you? Why are you doing this?"

"I'm Aaron Mortlock, and my plan is to free my brother, Shawn Mortlock."

A lead ball landed in her stomach. Shawn Mortlock was a small-scale domestic terrorist, who'd blown up a federal courthouse fourteen years ago. The only reason he wasn't on death row was that he'd picked a holiday, and the courthouse had been empty. His lawyer had argued that was intentional, that Shawn wasn't a killer, just an anarchist. The FBI thought he was both deadly and stupid, and they used his case in training classes.

Aaron was a criminal too, but not on the same scale. Yet the bureau had charged Aaron Mortlock with conspiracy to commit terrorist acts just for being connected to Shawn. In time, the director had dropped those charges in exchange for Aaron's testimony against three other white-collar criminals who'd been running bank fraud and extortion rackets. It had all taken place before her time at the bureau, but it was widely rumored that the terrorism charges against Aaron had been fabricated to pressure him to turn on his criminal ring. But obviously, the white-collar criminal in the family knew how to make explosives too.

She had to know what he had in mind. "You're going to use me to bomb a federal prison?"

He shook his head slowly, as if she were stupid. "Shawn is being transferred tomorrow, and we're going to intercept him."

Aaron's talk of sabotaging prison supply trucks suddenly made sense. He must have planned to use the inner circle to unwittingly help him free his brother, but Luke had rejected the idea. Now Aaron was using her. But why? Did he know she was a federal agent or was she just convenient?

"The others think we're going with them today on their mission, but we're not. Please keep your mouth shut about it." He held up a small black device that looked like a cell phone. "You're one push away from death."

So was he.

Another grim smile. "Yes, I'd get blown up too. But so would all your new friends. Or if you wait until we're out there on the road to make a move, the explosive could take out another car, like some sweet family of five. You're not going to let either of those things happen." He waved the gun at her again. "And don't forget this."

If things went south, she would take a bullet before hurting someone else—or letting a domestic terrorist escape. But she would go along with whatever he wanted up until that point. Somewhere along the way, she would find an opportunity to stop him. She just had to keep her mind and body strong. "I'd like a drink of water, and I need to use the bathroom." Her voice was scratchy.

"Not yet. When it's time to leave."

"I'd like the water now. My throat hurts."

"Too bad. I have little sympathy for federal spies."

So he did know. But how? She'd been so careful.

"What's your real name?"

She weighed the pros and cons of telling him. She needed him to trust her, or at least see her as human. Besides, what did it matter now? They were both likely to be dead before the day was over. Finally, she said, "Dallas."

"Just Dallas?"

"Yes."

"I like it. I grew up in Texas."

That explained a few things. "Does Luke know who you are?"

"Of course not." Aaron let out a disgusted sound. "Luke still likes this country and thinks he can change how the government works. He doesn't know how little chance he has."

They both became aware of movement in the house— Cree thumping down the stairs, and the front door opening.

"It's time." Aaron stood. "The story is that we hooked up last night and we're driving in together today. Luke won't like it, but he won't argue. He'll be too hurt."

"I should change. They'll think it's odd that I'm still in my running clothes."

"No changing clothes. You can use the bathroom in here, with me watching, and then we're heading out." Aaron put the gun to her head, while he ripped up the tape off her arms "Remember, you'll blow the whole house if you step out of line." He pointed to his workbench. "And I have a second bomb that's coming with us, in case you decide to commit heroic suicide. But please don't make me use it. Shawn has plans for it." Aaron chuckled again. "I almost didn't have enough for the second one after the stupid dog ate some of the glycol."

Treck.

Dallas wanted to head-butt him. Instead, she walked to the bathroom, moving slowly, painfully aware she probably wouldn't survive this day. But at least Drager would get his takedown.

Chapter 32

Luke stood in the shower, trying to clear his mind. He hadn't slept well, then he'd gotten up early and gone out for a bike ride and nearly been hit by a car. The encounter had unnerved him. Feeling jittery was the last thing he needed today, when they would be conducting their most important—and most dangerous—mission. He needed to be calm and confident, but his headspace was moving in the wrong direction. He couldn't stop thinking about Judge Bidwell taking millions of dollars to add years to prison sentences or incarcerate people when probation would have been more appropriate. The man was evil! Bidwell had even killed his court clerk to keep her from testifying. He knew it in his bones.

A scene played out in his head, where he confronted the judge and described in painful detail what prison was like for an eighteen-year-old kid. In his fantasy, he slammed the old man against a wall, got right in his face, and called him a maggot, a sociopath, and a killer. Luke had played out the confrontation over and over. Sometimes, he beat the judge with his fists, leaving him lying on the ground, crying like the cowardly piece of shit he was. But those mental exercises weren't satisfying. He needed to do it in person—but the judge was dead. So not fair! If anyone ever needed to spend time in prison, it was J.D. Bidwell.

What had he done with the money? Had he lived in a mansion and driven a Ferrari? Did he still have a shitload of cash in the bank? Another thought hit him. Had the judge's wife known about the payoffs? How could she not? Had she freely spent the blood money too?

Luke dressed and gathered what he needed for the day: cell phone, gloves, van key, and business credit card to keep stashed in the vehicle. What else? Instinct told him to leave his ID at home and refuse to speak if he was arrested. But that wasn't going to happen, he told himself. They'd done their homework, and they had the senator on the ropes.

A knock at his door startled him. He turned, taking a long breath to settle his nerves. Abby charged in. "Are you ready? This is going to be fun!" Her eyes danced with excitement. Before he could respond, she blurted, "This will be even better than skydiving or rock climbing, the ultimate adventure." Abby bounced on her feet as she talked.

Luke had never seen her like this. "It's not an adventure. We're not doing this for fun. I hope this isn't about the adrenaline rush for you."

"Oh please. You get off on the danger too. We all do."

He would never admit that, even to himself. "I'm having second thoughts about this mission. It crosses a line."

Abby lunged toward him, her face contorted with anger. "Don't you dare back out. This is our chance to take a giant step forward. Decriminalizing pot at the federal level is the cornerstone."

He knew she was right. But he finally realized what was going on. Abby was high. She was using again. *Oh god.* She'd probably started after she'd bought that meth for the failed mission to plant drugs on the governor. "You're blasted."

Luke sat down, feeling defeated. "I'm not sure we should do this while you're high."

"Don't say that." She softened her tone. "I would never use again. I just had too much coffee."

"Okay." He didn't believe her, but there was no point in arguing. He headed to the door, rushed into Abby's room and looked around. She was right behind him, shouting and pounding his back. "What are you doing? Get out!"

Luke didn't see any obvious signs of drug use. No needles or cotton balls or small mirrors with a light dusting of white powder. But Abby was smart enough to hide them, and he didn't have time to search every drawer and container. If they still planned to hit the senator's house today during their narrow window of opportunity, it was time to leave. He spun around to face Abby. "This issue isn't over. We'll deal with it later. But if you're using, you'll have to leave. We'll pay for rehab if we can."

"There is no issue!"

"I hope not. Let Cree know he's riding with you, then get in the van. I'm taking my own truck." Luke pounded up the stairs and knocked on Tara's door. She didn't respond. He rapped it again. "Hey, it's time. We're leaving soon." He moved next door to Aaron's room and did the same.

Aaron opened the door a few inches, looking haggard, the gray under his eyes more pronounced. "I'm ready," Aaron said. "I'll be down in a bit."

"Hey, did you find Judge Bidwell's address for me?" He'd asked Aaron about it the night before but hadn't indicated it was important. Now Luke was in a hurry to know.

"It's in Silver Spring, 1652 Highland." Aaron grinned through the narrow opening. "Don't do anything stupid."

Good advice. Could he follow it? "Hey, have you seen

Tara?" Luke glanced next door, expecting her to step out any moment.

"She's with me." Aaron shifted on his feet and glanced away. "We kinda hooked up, and she's going to ride with me."

What? A jolt of jealousy seized him. He'd thought Tara was into him. "That's unexpected," he finally said. "As long as she does her job as lookout on the other end of the street."

"Don't worry, she will."

"Okay, but let's roll." Luke walked away, feeling more rattled than before. Tara and Aaron. He wouldn't have predicted that in a million years. It must have been a pity fuck. Tara had felt sorry for the older guy because his days were numbered. Luke tried to forget it. He had to stay focused on the mission.

Downstairs, he filled a thermos of water and grabbed an apple from the fridge, then went outside. Abby and Cree stood next to the van arguing about who would drive. "Cree's driving," Luke announced. "End of discussion." He snatched the keys from Abby's hand. The van had been purchased with money from the private donor, but it was registered under Cree's name. He'd bought the truck from Hana but left it in her name. Luke had never adopted an alias, but he was off the grid and didn't use his name on any paperwork.

"Fuck you!" Abby climbed in the passenger's side.

Another wave of doubt rolled over him. "Cree, I think Abby's high. And I'm nervous about doing this mission with her."

Cree's shoulders fell. "Are you sure? Maybe it's just adrenaline."

"Possibly. But she's been irritable and moody lately and we don't really need her today."

"Which is why I'm not worried." His young friend

shrugged. "Abby's part isn't critical. But we can't back out. This is our biggest shot at a legislative change."

"I just thought you had a right to know my concerns."

"That's cool."

"Are the coveralls in the van?"

"Yes they are." Cree put up his fist for a bump. "Let's do this."

Luke bumped back, then headed for his truck. After starting the engine, he looked up at the house. Were Aaron and Tara coming? Next to him, Cree backed the van out and started down the drive. Luke backed up too, watching the entry. The door opened and Tara stepped out. She saw him looking and gave a small wave. No smile though.

He waved back and shifted gears. Did Tara regret her hookup with Aaron? Maybe she was nervous about the mission too. Any rational person would be. He wondered how long Tara would stay with the group. Now that they knew they could trust her, it was time to let her get her car and move in a few more personal things.

Or maybe they should disband for a while after their big win today. The feds would double their effort to find them. And with their main donation cut off and Abby relapsed, it would be a good time to give up the farmhouse, go their separate ways, and lay low for a while. Luke decided to make the announcement that evening. He pressed the gas and followed the van down the driveway, but he couldn't shake the feeling that everything felt wrong.

Forty minutes later, when he crossed the river into DC, he called Cree. It took the other driver a while to answer. "Hey, what's up?"

"I've changed my mind. I don't think we should do this

mission."

A pause. "Are you afraid to go back to prison?"

Hell yes, he was afraid. "I just have a bad feeling about today. Too many things feel off to me."

"Hang on a minute." In the background, Cree told Abby what Luke had just said.

She responded loud enough for him to hear. "Too bad. We're going anyway."

Cree cut in. "I'm with Abby. We're going ahead. Especially if Aaron and Tara still have our backs."

"You'll have to ask them. Tara is riding with Aaron."

"I'll call him now," Cree said. Another pause. "I don't blame you for not wanting to take the risk. None of us did ten years, and we won't face the same sentence as you."

The unspoken reality. Because he was mixed race and darker skinned, he would be punished more harshly. "Thanks for understanding. But I'm not afraid just for myself. I just don't think we should do a home invasion. Because that's what the feds will call it, even if it's just a dog in the house."

"I disagree. It's a B&E at most," Cree asserted. "The senator won't even press charges if he wants to keep the child porn suppressed."

Luke was done arguing. "It's your decision. I'm out."

A long moment of silence. "Are you going back home?"

"No, I need some closure with Bidwell and possibly his wife. Be safe." Luke hung up and set the GPS in his car to find the judge's address.

Chapter 33

"You're driving." Aaron nudged her toward the car with the end of his handgun. Being at the wheel was good, Dallas decided. Her hands would be free, and she would be in control. She could plow his side of the vehicle into a tree at the first opportunity. Which might set off the bomb unless she managed to get out.

At the last moment, Aaron said, "I changed my mind, you'll ride shotgun."

Every nerve in her body screamed, *Don't get in the car!* In college, when she'd watched thriller movies, she'd mentally yelled at anyone who climbed into a vehicle at gunpoint. Women especially—if the bad guy was a rapist or a serial killer and someone was nearby to call for help. People survived gunshot wounds every day. But no one survived an explosive going off under their jacket. And if Aaron used the gun, the bullet would enter her brain, killing her instantly. She had no options.

Aaron pulled a roll of duct tape from his bulky jacket and held it out to her. "Tape your wrists together."

He had the detonator in one hand, the tape in the other, and the gun in his waistband. Was this her chance? Grabbing the detonator could set off the bomb. What would happen if she knocked it out of his hand?

"Don't even think about it."

As he spoke, she lunged forward, bringing up her forearm to slam into his. A searing pain sliced down her arm, stopping her momentum. Aaron yelled, "On your knees or I'll cut your throat next."

Blood gushed from her forearm, and Dallas gritted her teeth. Where had the knife come from? His sleeve? Not wanting to get stabbed again and left in the driveway to bleed to death, Dallas dropped down, gravel grinding into her flesh.

"Use the tape to stop the bleeding first," Aaron commanded. "Then tape your wrists together. Do the best you can, and I'll secure it."

Dallas wiped the oozing blood on her pants to dry the five-inch wound as best she could. The cut wasn't deep, but the pain would make her slower and more cautious, and that was his point. She wrapped the tape around her forearm a few times, then used her teeth to tear off the strip. Binding her own wrists was more challenging, but she kept the tape loose and left the roll hanging.

Aaron cut the roll free and pocketed it. "Get in the car."

Dallas complied. He probably wouldn't kill her until he was done using her, but she didn't want to die slowly from a dozen painful injuries. She'd rather go out all at once, in a heroic move. And the most important thing she could do would be to take out Shawn Mortlock. Assholes who blew up government buildings were the worst of the worst. If she died right here, right now, Aaron might kidnap someone else and still be able to free his brother. If Shawn escaped, hundreds of citizens might die in his next attack. As long as she had breath and fight left in her body, she wasn't going to let that happen.

Chapter 34

Drager checked the Real Food blog again, but Dallas hadn't posted. It was time to head to Senator Pearlman's house. Most of the team was already in place, and the three agents in the house had been there since before daylight that morning. Drager had been waiting to see if he would hear from his UC, but he hadn't. He had to assume the takedown was still a go. If not, they would waste their time, but no harm done. Unless the inner circle changed their plans and struck somewhere else. Dallas would have warned him though—assuming that she could.

This time, when he entered the neighborhood, he parked across the street and two houses down, tucking in behind a big SUV. A few other cars surrounded the next house, and he hoped to blend with the family-car crowd. He was the last agent to arrive because his role was less critical. As the team leader—and the old man in the crowd—he was happy to let others play key parts, then go in after the fact to mop up. Drager shut off the car, rolled down the window a few inches, and scrunched low in the seat. At least the bureau still sprang for comfortable cars. The team had discussed using a fully equipped van, but it would have stood out anywhere in the neighborhood. Because the inner circle used a phony work van, they would have noticed it for sure.

The sky grew dark and the wind picked up. Was the first fall storm finally rolling in? They'd had a light rain on Monday, but the temperature hadn't even dropped, so it didn't count. Today was starting to look ominous. He hoped the activists didn't have second thoughts and change their plans.

After a few minutes of waiting, his phone beeped and he glanced at it. A text message from Jocelyn, asking him and another person to run a license number. *What was that about?* Staying low in the car, Drager called the plate into his field office and stayed on the line until he got an answer. Hana Kasumi. Wasn't that the woman who owned the farmhouse? His neck nerves tingled. She was in Japan, so who was driving the vehicle? Luke Maddox? And where had Jocelyn seen it?

He started to call but heard a loud V-8 engine coming down the street. A white van with blue lettering. This was it. He felt his heart beating in his throat. No matter how many times he'd done this over the years, confrontations still made him nervous. A man was behind the wheel of the van, but it wasn't Maddox. The driver was younger with a narrow face and long straight hair. Cree Songchild. In the passenger's seat was a woman. Tall and thin with short dark hair. Abby Gleeson. How many members were in the back? Would they bring another vehicle?

Drager clicked on his radio. "They're here. Two in the front of the van, so far."

"Copy that," Agent Manning answered from inside the house.

Agent Wunn, who was walking the block with a stroller, came back, "Sorry I missed them."

"We're good."

The van pulled into the Pearlmans' driveway. For three long minutes, nothing happened. Drager's lungs ached from holding his breath. Finally, the van doors opened, and the two people in front climbed out. They wore blue jumpsuits and leather tool belts. The van's side door stayed closed. Drager touched his talk button. "They're coming to the door. Two subjects. No obvious weapons."

Where the hell was Dallas? And what about Maddox? Drager scanned up and down the street for a second vehicle and didn't see anything new. Tension mounted in his chest, and he reached for his interior handle. He wanted to bust their leader more than anything. At the front door of the house, Songchild seemed to fiddle with something in his hands, then a minute later, the two went in. Drager bolted from his car and charged across the street.

* * *

The minute they were inside, Cree got a bad feeling. The house was spacious and beautiful and reminded him of the home he'd grown up in. Suddenly, it seemed wrong to be here. He grabbed Abby's arm. "Let's just get the dog and go. We'll call the senator from the road."

She jerked free. "We have to get his laptop too. We need the child porn pictures to keep him in line."

Cree's anger at Luke surfaced again. "We need another person." Aaron and Tara had flaked off too, not even returning his calls. He couldn't believe the whole damn crew had abandoned him. Except Abby, of course. She was loyal and true, even if she was using. More so than Luke. What had happened to him?

"We'll be fine," Abby countered. "I'll get the dog, take some video, and call the senator, while you find the laptop. Let's go." She trotted toward the sound of whimpering in the back of the house.

Cree started after her. In the hall, he opened a door on the left, looking for an office or study, but it was a bathroom. At the end of the long hall, a woman with a small dog in her arms stepped out of a side room. "What are you doing here?" She seemed oddly calm.

Oh shit! The wife wasn't supposed to be home. Cree reached for Abby's arm to grab her and run. But Abby lunged forward, then pulled a gun from under her jacket. She pointed it at Mrs. Pearlman. "Give us the dog and the senator's laptop!"

What the hell was she doing? Cree wanted no part of it. He turned to run. A man in a suit blocked his path. The agent also had a weapon, and it was pointed at his head.

"Hands in the air!"

Cree did as he was told. His parents would hire a great lawyer, and he would get out of this okay. Shouts echoed behind him. Moments later, a gunshot blasted through the hallway.

No! Instinctively, he dropped to the floor, his hands still above him.

Another suited man rushed in from the front of the house. "Who's down?"

"The target," a voice called out.

* * *

While a team agent cuffed Songchild, Drager rushed past them. The body on the floor at the midway point was Abby

Gleeson. Thank goodness. Agent Manning stood over her, and Stella Pearlman was upright at the end of the hall, clutching the little dog. *Why was she in the open?* "Are you all right?"

"I'm fine. A little shaky though. She had a gun. I didn't know they would have guns."

Drager mentally kicked himself. Why hadn't he seen Gleeson's gun when she climbed from the van? Was it his damn left eye? "We didn't expect them to be armed either. Our intel indicated otherwise. I'm sorry."

A third agent came pounding down a flight of stairs. "Everyone all right?"

"Yes." Drager kneeled next to Gleeson and checked for a pulse. She was definitely dead. A young woman with a passion for the wrong things. He didn't have time yet to process the full explanation for why it had happened on his watch.

"Where is the UC?" Manning asked.

"I don't know." Drager heard a hint of panic in his own voice. He turned to Cree Songchild, now in cuffs. "Where is Luke Maddox?"

The man swallowed hard. "I think he went to see Judge Bidwell's widow."

What? "To kill her?"

"No!" Songchild scowled. "No one was supposed to get hurt. I didn't know Abby had a gun, I swear."

"Where are Aaron Foster and Tara Adams?"

"I don't know. They were supposed to be here."

Drager scrambled to make sense of what was happening. A growing dread told him Dallas was in trouble. He had to get out of this hallway and away from Abby's dead body. Drager strode out of the house, taking gulps of fresh air. Where would Foster and Dallas go? To hit another target? Which one?

His phone conversation with Dallas last Monday came back to him in a rush. She'd mentioned prison supply trucks. *Oh dear god.* What if Aaron Foster really was Aaron Mortlock, and the WITSEC program was wrong about his death? Shawn Mortlock was in a Virginia federal prison a couple hundred miles southeast. Aaron Mortlock could be on his way to break him out. Fearing the worst, Drager wouldn't let himself think about Dallas.

He pulled his cell phone and called the bureau's headquarters. "Agent Drager. I need to talk to the assistant director if he's available. If not, put me through to Critical Incident Operations."

Special Agent Duvall, the CIO commander came on the line. "What's the situation?"

"A possible prison break. Shawn Mortlock at Lee federal. His brother Aaron may be en route there now, and we need agents on the ground at every point along the way."

"Where is the intel coming from?" Duvall was deadpan, but Drager understood his skepticism.

He swallowed hard. "A female UC embedded with an activist group. She might be with Aaron Mortlock, so proceed with caution."

"She went rogue?"

"No. She's likely being held against her will." *If she wasn't dead.*

"Where did they start from? Virginia covers a lot of territory."

"Butts Corner, southeast of Fairfax Station. Alert the prison as well." Central command at headquarters would have more success reaching the right people inside the prison.

"Copy that." The CIO commander hung up.

Some of the tension left his body. Duvall would contact agents with the right specialties and get them into a command center to handle the situation. Drager mentally chastised himself. Why hadn't he seen this coming? For starters, WITSEC had told him Aaron Mortlock was dead. And Dallas had given him the green light for the takedown at the senator's home. Drager knew he'd acted on the best information he had. Now he prayed, without faith, that Dallas would be all right. Virginia field agents would get to the scene before he did, and there was nothing he could do but wait it out. Except drive to Judge Bidwell's house and arrest Luke Maddox—if he was still there.

Drager ducked back in the house, updated Agent Wunn, and ran to his car.

Chapter 35

Ninety minutes earlier

Jocelyn washed down the last bite of her breakfast bar with Mountain Dew and vowed to cut back on the stuff. But she had to find another source of caffeine first. She couldn't drink coffee or hot tea because they made her sweat, and she didn't trust energy drinks. Who knew what they really put in them? So that didn't leave much—except the groggy feeling she tended to have during and after a night-shift rotation. With her usual good intentions, she filled a water bottle for later, then conducted a check before she left the house: service weapon, cell phone, shoulder bag, and car keys. She was ready.

But first she had to call Eastern National Bank. She pulled her laptop back out of her bag, logged into a search engine, then keyed the number into her phone. She would add it to her notes later. When a receptionist answered, she asked to speak to Joan Bidwell, not really expecting her to be there. The widow was likely taking time off to grieve. But Jocelyn had driven out to her home late yesterday afternoon, and no one had been there. So she was being proactive about not wasting her time again.

"Mrs. Bidwell isn't here this morning, but she'll be in this afternoon for a board meeting."

"Thanks." Jocelyn hung up. This conversation couldn't wait.

In the car, she laid her phone in her lap, clicked over to speaker mode, and called Sergeant Danner. He didn't answer, so she left a message. "I'm heading to Judge Bidwell's house to talk to his wife. I know the team interviewed her after her husband's death, but I need to follow up with questions about Callie Sayers. I'll be in later." She called her partner next.

It took him a while to answer and he sounded weak. "Snyder speaking."

"It's Jocelyn. Did you find Sherry Jones, the prostitute?"

"Not yet. But I called motor vehicles, and she replaced her license two days ago, so we know she's out there."

Good news. Jocelyn had begun to worry the hooker would turn up dead. "Watch your email for the victim's credit card records and check Tuesday night. If there's anything interesting, call me." She backed out of the garage.

"You're not coming in?"

"I'm interviewing Mrs. Bidwell this morning and want to catch her at home. Since I can't question the judge, she's the next best thing. And oddly enough, she seems to have called our victim not long before her death. I want to ask her about that."

"You think she might be the killer? Should I join you?"

"No, stay on the financial records."

"Check back with me after you talk to her, okay?"

Jocelyn suppressed a chuckle. "She's a sixty-year-old banker, so I'm not worried about my safety. But I suspect she knows more about both deaths than she's admitted. Talk to you later." She hung up, reached for her vapor, and inhaled her first hit of nicotine for the day. She would have to cut down on that soon too.

The Bidwells lived in Park View, right next to a golf course. Jocelyn didn't envy their massive house with the guest cottage in back, but she would have killed for access to the greens. She loved golf but hated driving to the range and had quit the sport for lack of time when Kyle was growing up and she'd had to attend his weekend sports instead. She made a decision. That's what she would do with her free time now. Get back out on the green. Her sister would love it. To hell with the glass blowing. Jocelyn pulled into the long driveway and forced herself to focus. Another vehicle, a midsize black truck, was already there.

She walked slowly past it, looking inside, an occupational habit. The pickup was old and dented and looked out of place in front of the million-dollar home. A yard-care person? She grabbed her cell phone, keyed the license plate into a text message, then added: *Who is this?* She sent the message to Detective Snyder, then added her ex-husband to the queue. Sometimes the feds had faster access to information.

Jocelyn walked up the flagstone path to the double front doors and noticed one was ajar. Raised voices echoed from the interior. Jocelyn shoved her jacket flap behind her weapon so she could access the gun more easily, then pushed open the unlatched door. Stepping into a white-stone foyer, she moved toward the voices, grateful for her quiet work shoes. The sounds came from the kitchen, on the other side of a spacious living area, and she heard someone mention the judge. She quickened her pace. The witness she'd come to question could be in danger, and her duty to protect justified her presence in the house.

As she approached, she spotted two people talking at a

table in a breakfast nook. A tall older woman with short dyed-brown hair and a muscular man in his early thirties. They were both too emotionally engaged to notice her, but their voices were loud enough to be heard clearly.

Joan Bidwell cried as she talked. "You're right. I did know about the payoffs. Not at first, but eventually J.D. told me. He said he took the money partly because I earned so much more than he did."

"Why didn't you report him or make him stop? Hundreds of lives were ruined!" The man was upset, but held on to his dignity.

"I couldn't turn my husband in and watch him go to jail, but he promised me it was over, and I believed him. For a while." Mrs. Bidwell put her hands to her face in obvious shame. "I'm so sorry. I've tried to make up for it. Not just for you, but for everyone he hurt."

"How? What are you talking about?" The man slumped back in his chair.

Jocelyn's cell phone vibrated silently in her pocket. She slipped it out and glanced at the message. It was from Ross: *Truck is registered to Hana Kasumi but driver could be Luke Maddox.* The top suspect in the judge's murder. Jocelyn unholstered her weapon but kept it at her side and didn't move. She wanted to hear everything.

Mrs. Bidwell finally said, "I donated a lot of money to Justice Reform Now, then I supported your group generously for the last year and a half."

Maddox sat up, mouth open. "You're the anonymous donor?"

"Yes, but I have to stop now." Joan Bidwell leaned forward, her voice desperate. "You can never tell anyone about the donations."

"Why stop? We have so much more to accomplish."

For a long moment, she was quiet, twisting the ring on her hand. "Because J.D. is dead, and the police are asking questions. And the IRS froze our accounts. And because my family owns a big chunk of CSA, and they're going to be investigated next."

"The judge was taking bribes from a company you own?" Maddox raised his voice to a new level of volume and disbelief.

"I don't own it directly!" Joan Bidwell started to cry again. "I'm so sorry about all this. But now that you've got your closure, you should go."

Maddox didn't move. "The judge killed his clerk, didn't he?"

"Of course he did. J.D. was worried about her testimony because he thought she might have kept records." She let out a bitter laugh. "I'm also sure the police will never prove it. He knew how to destroy evidence."

Jocelyn wished she could get out her recorder, but she wasn't willing to put away her weapon.

"The judge should have gone to prison," Maddox cried out. "Who the hell killed him?"

A loud sob escaped her, but Joan Bidwell didn't answer at first. After another long moment, she said, "I couldn't let J.D. go to trial. Too much would have come out, and I could have lost my position at the bank."

Maddox was on his feet. "You killed him? Your own husband?"

"He deserved to die. He was heartless. You know that as well as anyone."

Holy shit! Jocelyn's pulse escalated, and she took a step forward without meaning to.

They both turned to look at her, and she brought up her weapon. "Get on the ground! You're under arrest."

Joan Bidwell slipped from her chair to her knees and raised her hands. She was crying too hard to speak.

The man didn't move. He stared at Jocelyn long and hard.

Don't come at me, she pleaded silently. "Get on the ground! Hands in the air!"

Maddox turned and ran for the sliding door. *Shit!* She couldn't shoot an unarmed man in the back, and she couldn't chase him either. Not with a confessed killer right there who needed to be cuffed. Jocelyn called dispatch. He wouldn't get far.

Chapter 36

The lush green countryside kept rolling by, but its tranquility was lost on Dallas. Her mind worked overtime, playing out scenarios in which she tried to save herself—while keeping Shawn from escaping. With her wrists duct-taped together and the bomb still strapped to her stomach, she had to fight off panic. The bureau wasn't coming to her rescue. Drager and his team were at Senator Pearlman's, arresting the inner circle. Drager would be alarmed by her disappearance, but he would have no way of connecting the Aaron Foster alias to Shawn Mortlock. The best she could hope for was that the bureau had put out a statewide alert for Aaron's car—and didn't think she'd gone rogue.

"Do you have a family?" Aaron's question surprised her. He'd been silent for most of the drive.

"Not much. Why?" She had no desire to chat with him, but if it helped make him see her as a human worthy of life, then she would say anything.

"Any brothers to carry on the family name?"

"No, but in my case, that's probably a good thing." Her parents shouldn't have been allowed to breed, and she couldn't believe she'd turned out to be so law-abiding. If she had a brother, he would probably be in jail.

"You have no loyalty." Aaron sounded disappointed. "I

had hoped you would understand why I can't let Shawn die in prison."

"I do understand. Didn't you say you'd promised your mother?"

"That I did, and I'm a man of my word."

Yeah, right. "Does your mom know you're dying?"

"Of course. That's why Shawn is so important now." Aaron shook his head. "The one kid I have is a girl, who got married, changed her name, and disowned all of us."

Smart woman. "You live as Aaron Foster now, so the family name can't be that big of a deal."

He snapped his head toward her, eyes flashing. "That was temporary! Witness protection assigned it to me, but it's not real. It's not who I am."

He was in WITSEC? How had Drager missed that? "How did you end up with the inner circle?" She remembered the story he'd told her last time. A load of bull.

"I needed a new place to hide out, and they seemed useful." Aaron changed the subject. "How did you end up in the FBI?"

"I wish you would get over that idea and let me go."

"I saw your message on the Real Food blog. That's what tipped me off. Plus the call to a cash-only phone."

Had he spied on everything she'd done? Aaron had more hacking skills than he'd let on to the inner circle. "That's a lot of conjecture. Have you considered taking medication for your paranoia?" She tried to sound sincere but knew it didn't matter now.

He laughed. "You're good, but you're wasting your talents for the wrong team."

Aaron turned off to yet another back road. She hadn't seen any traffic in the last twenty minutes, and she didn't expect to see any along this route. Would a prison transfer van come through here? Did they take back roads on purpose? After a minute, Aaron pulled off at a break in the trees, took his laptop from under the seat, and searched online for something.

"Checking on the transfer van?"

"It's on schedule." He gave her a sly grin. "Hacking into prison systems is relatively easy. I'm surprised it doesn't happen more often." He pulled back onto the road, one hand on the steering wheel, the other on the detonator. The gun was in his lap.

Dallas' chest tightened. They must be close to the interception site. What the hell was his plan?

The asphalt narrowed and passed through a series of rock cliffs. After a long slow curve, Aaron braked and coasted to a stop, half off the road. He parked, shut off the engine, and popped the hood latch. "Stay put, okay?" Aaron climbed out and propped open the hood, then came around to her side of the car. "Now you can get out."

Her legs trembled as they hit the ground. Instinct told her to run—to get as far away as she could, as fast as she could. But she couldn't outrun a bullet or a click of a switch. Her feet, still in their running shoes from the evening before, still itched to move. Going out for a jog had been her last act of free will.

Pepper spray! She'd tucked it into her yoga pants pocket like always before her run. Had Aaron searched her while she slept and taken it or was it still there? If she could get her hands free . . .

Aaron cut into her thoughts. "After I remove the tape, I want you to lie down in the road, like you're hurt."

"You think the driver will stop?"

"A bleeding woman on the road? Of course he will."
Aaron started cutting the duct tape from her wrists.

"Then what?"

"Just stay down and you won't get hurt."

Lying piece of shit. He would shoot her right after he shot
the van driver and the guard accompanying him. Unless one
of them managed to shoot him first. Aaron thought he would
have the element of surprise, but the prison employees
would be on alert for anything that looked like a trap or an
assault. Wouldn't they? Unless he'd bribed someone, which
was probably why Shawn Mortlock was being transferred.

"Move!" Aaron pushed her toward the road.

She hurried out of his reach, tension making her ache.
Confronting him now would result in a bullet in her brain,
and she really would bleed on the road. Her forearm had quit
dripping, but she still had blood smeared all over it. Dallas
reached the asphalt and turned around. Aaron shuffled
toward her, breathing hard.

"Any particular place?"

"Right there is fine, but we need more blood."

Oh shit.

He stepped up, still holding the gun in one hand and the
device in the other. "Rub that cut and make it bleed."

Dallas pressed her thumb into the wound and bore down,
clenching her teeth, more in anger than in pain.

"Now wipe the blood on your shirt."

While she rubbed her arm against her chest, careful to
avoid the explosive, the pasty son-of-a-bitch smashed his gun
into her forehead. Shards of pain stabbed into her eyes, and
she clouded over for a second. Forehead throbbing, she
tightened her hands into fists. Every fiber in her body wanted
to lash out and hurt the little fucker. She visualized punching

him in the throat just to keep herself calm. Warm blood oozed down her nose and over her lip.

"You can lay down now."

Dallas lowered herself to the ground, plotting her next move. As soon as she heard a shot, she would roll to the other side of the road, then take cover behind the prison van. Or make a break for the trees. With her hands free now, she had more options. She might even be able to rip off the explosive while Aaron tried to free his brother. She'd been trapped in a room once with a man who threatened to set off a bomb, but this time, no sharpshooters were out there waiting to take him out.

"Try to look injured," he commanded. "Maybe bend one of your legs."

She went along, hoping he would eventually walk away. She assumed Aaron would hide behind his car.

The road was cool and hard under her back. Her forehead hurt and blood continued to flow, only now it trickled down the left side of her face and into her hair. Wind roared in the trees, rustling the crisp fall leaves. In the distance, the gushing sound of a river played softly like background music.

How long would she have to lie here? What if the prison van was late? Or changed its route?

A moment later, she had the answer. An engine rumbled in the distance, and the road under her hummed with a growing vibration. Her pulse jumped a notch, and she could feel throbbing in her throat. Would this be her last experience? The most fucked-up adventure of all? She said a silent goodbye to Cameron, her long-time friend and lover, a man of endless patience and inner tranquility. Qualities she loved him for, yet resented too. He deserved better, and now he would be free to find that person.

Shut up and focus!

The roar of the engine grew loud, and the road hummed. She braced for the worst. Once the van rounded the corner, it had little time to stop, depending on its speed. She had to be ready to roll out of its way. Would she blow herself up doing that?

What if the driver didn't stop? If she moved too soon, he would see that she wasn't injured and know it was trap. Would he run over her to protect himself and keep his prisoner secure? Would Aaron or the guard shoot her if she moved?

Another thought hit her. Aaron might detonate the bomb as soon as the van got close. The explosion would probably knock out the driver and send the vehicle off the road. But his brother would likely survive. Or was that too risky for him? She was fucked either way. The engine roared around the corner and Dallas held her breath.

Oh god, the van wasn't stopping.

Chapter 37

Aaron held his breath as the squeal of brakes ripped through the air. He wanted to go now! Just run and shoot and get it over with. But he made himself wait. He needed at least one of the guards to get out of the van and leave himself open. The squealing continued, and he smelled burning rubber. Leaning forward, he peeked around the back of the car. The van screeched to a stop, and the air was suddenly quiet. To avoid hitting the woman, the prison vehicle had pulled off the road on this side. Perfect. His targets were closer than he'd expected.

The crunch of metal on metal pinged through the silence. The front passenger's door was open. Aaron slipped the detonator into his pocket and counted slowly—a thousand and one, a thousand and two, a thousand and go! He charged from behind the car, both hands on the Glock, and fired chest level at the dark uniform. One, two, three quick shots. The man staggered back and slammed into the van as he pulled the trigger. Aaron shifted his gaze and weapon as he ran toward the driver, firing three more shots. One round of return fire zinged past him. The windshield shattered, and he fired another round through it. But he didn't see the driver. Had he ducked down? Or slid out?

Movement to the right caught his eye. The fed was up and

running. *Shit!* He took aim, squeezed the trigger, and struck her in the shoulder. She stumbled forward. Aaron spun back toward the van. Where was the driver?

After the deafening gunfire, the scene was silent again. He jogged to the van, lungs aching from the exertion. Through the open door, he saw the driver slumped over, hanging from his safety belt off the side of his seat. Aaron put a bullet into the driver's head for good measure, then jogged back to the guard on the ground in front of the vehicle. He put a bullet between his eyes as well, then unclipped the guard's keys and shuffled to the back of the van. He opened both doors, pulled in some oxygen, and climbed in.

"Aaron! You did it!" Shawn beamed at him from a side bench.

The sight of his younger brother filled him with a strange joy, and he heard his mother call out *My boy!* Aaron kissed Shawn's forehead and handed him the keys. "Get yourself unlocked. I have to check on something."

Aaron climbed out, hoping it was the last strenuous thing he had to for a long time. Maybe ever. He pushed himself to hurry to the front of the van. The fed struggled to get up. He pulled the detonator out of his pocket.

Chapter 38

Dallas struggled to her feet, but her head was spinning and she thought she would vomit. The pain in her shoulder burned like a branding iron that had somehow penetrated to the bone. *Suck it up,* she told herself. She breathed deeply and started to run, reaching to pull off her jacket. She had to get the damn explosive off her body.

A bony hand grabbed her injured shoulder and squeezed. Tiny white stars danced around her peripheral vision, and she blacked out for a moment. When she opened her eyes, she was on her knees again, and Aaron stood over her. "Get up and walk to the car."

"Why? It's over. Just leave me here."

"It's not over until Shawn and I are out of the state." Aaron reached down and grabbed her in the pit of her uninjured arm. "Let's go." His effort was weak, and Dallas had to push herself to her feet again. What now? She didn't want to go anywhere with the psycho brothers, but she wasn't ready to die either.

The dead guard on the gravel caught her eye, and she cringed. *God dammit!* Could she have stopped this hijack? Not with an explosive device strapped to her stomach. But she might still have a chance to keep the brothers from getting away. She knew it was a bullshit hope and stupid hero thinking. She had to focus on staying alive. The bureau would catch the Mortlock brothers. They might be searching already.

Another man intercepted them on the way to the car. He was bigger than Aaron, but they shared the same narrow eyes and protruding brow. "Who the fuck is this?" The man in the gray prison uniform looked her over with a mix of anger and lust.

Dread filled her belly and rose in her throat. Dallas leaned forward and vomited up stomach bile.

"A federal agent with a gel-based explosive strapped to her. That's why you're a free man."

Shawn Mortlock grinned. "You kidnapped a federal agent? Brother, you have redeemed yourself."

"Let's get out of here." Aaron dragged Dallas to the car and shoved her in the back seat. Her shoulder burned with pain as he wrapped duct tape around it. At least the binding would slow the flow of blood. Sort of.

"Why are we keeping her?" Shawn climbed behind the wheel.

"Insurance," Aaron said, getting in the other side. "In case the feds are looking for my car. They'll let us get away rather than risk blowing up one of their own."

"Then we'll swap out this piece of shit as soon as we can." Shawn started the engine and gunned the car toward the road.

Dallas closed her eyes, feeling lightheaded. How much blood had she lost? The wound wasn't fatal, she could tell, but she needed medical attention. A bitter laugh died in her throat. The bomb was the real concern. Her jacket was still hanging from her shoulders, so she pulled it all the way off. With it out of the way, she could start peeling off the duct tape that was holding the explosive in place—if they didn't look back and pay attention to her. And if Aaron didn't tape her hands.

He glanced over the seat and said, "Don't be stupid. I will shoot you again."

She didn't respond or look at him.

Behind the wheel, Shawn let out a cry of joy. "I'm free! I'm driving." He turned to his brother and squeezed his shoulder. "Thank you, man. Does Mom know about this?"

"Not specifically. But I promised her I would get you out." Aaron finally turned back to the front. "We can't go to Mom's. It's the first place they'll look."

"I know that." Shawn gunned the engine again.

Dallas put their banter on a back burner, hearing the words but only focusing on a few details. With her right shoulder still throbbing, she put her left hand behind her back and felt under her shirt for the edge of the duct tape. After a few tries, she found it. With slow awkward movements, she began to peel, watching Aaron's head for movement.

Two minutes later, he turned to check, and she let her hand flop. This would take too damn long. Dallas tried not to despair. Maybe prison officials, or possibly fellow agents, were looking for them already.

After twenty minutes of traveling, while she made slow painful progress on the tape around her stomach, the vehicle slowed. "Look, another car is coming." Shawn seemed both eager and agitated.

Dallas snapped her head up to look out the front windshield. The landscape had changed, and they were headed down a gentle, winding slope, with views of the valley below. A low cement bridge came into sight, with a dark narrow river below it.

"We'll stop them and take their vehicle," Aaron said. "The sooner we get out of this one, the better."

"We can lose the hostage too." Shawn glanced over his shoulder at her.

Dallas hoped they wouldn't kill the other driver. They reached the bottom of the slope, and the road flattened out. The river crossing was up ahead, past a long grove of trees. She couldn't see the approaching car, but it had to be coming. When they reached the middle of the bridge, Shawn slowed, turned the car sideways, and shut it off.

The other vehicle had just crossed onto the bridge, and the driver slammed his brakes, stopping ten feet away.

"Your ride is over," Aaron said, looking back at her with a sick smile. "Get out."

The explosive was still strapped to her, with only about six inches of tape hanging down her back. Dallas climbed from the car, racking her brain for ideas. She glanced over at the other vehicle. *Oh god,* a minivan with a family. "Don't hurt them," she pleaded.

Shawn came around the car, grabbed her wounded shoulder, and dragged her to the wall of the bridge. It was only three feet tall, but thick enough to stand on. "Give me your gun, Aaron."

His brother didn't respond. He was watching the minivan. "Let's get the other people out here first. We don't know who they are. And they might be making a phone call right now." He held up his device and shouted at Dallas. "Come with me and don't do anything stupid, or I'll use you to blow them up."

She couldn't let that happen. Dallas hugged the side of the

bridge and took a step sideways. The brothers were now standing in front of their car about five feet away.

"Let me handle this!" Shawn grabbed the Glock from Aaron.

Dallas knew what was coming next. She shoved her hand into her pocket and pulled out the pepper spray.

Shawn spun and took a step toward her, jerking the weapon up into position. She aimed the little canister at his face and sprayed, her shoulder screaming in pain. At the same time, she swung her good arm up and grabbed the wrist that held the gun.

The pepper burned his eyes and Shawn let out a loud bellow.

Dallas kept spraying with one hand and squeezing his wrist with the other, her own eyes watering with pain. Shawn started to kick, but she jumped back, pulling his arm with her. The gun dropped to the ground. Still bellowing, Shawn's hands went to his eyes. Behind him, Aaron was coming at her.

Dallas scooped up the weapon and fired at Shawn's head. She squeezed the trigger again, but the magazine was empty.

"You bitch!" Aaron shouted and lunged at her, the detonator in his hand.

She had only once chance to survive. Dallas spun and vaulted over the thick cement wall. She plunged down, feet first, begging the universe for a short drop. The cold air of the river rushed up to meet her, and a moment later, she knifed through the icy water. For a split second, the impact made her think the bomb had exploded and she was gone. But she kept going and her feet hit bottom. Where was Aaron? Would the explosive go off under water?

Dallas discovered the gun was still in her hand. Thank

god. The family would be safe. Lungs bursting and her body frigid with shock, she wanted to push straight back up and surface for oxygen. But the river was pulling her downstream, and she went with the flow, hoping to get out of detonation range.

Chapter 39

Agent Grimes careened down the hill. He had passed the prison vehicle about twenty minutes back, stunned to see the two guards dead and the prisoner gone. The blood on the road in front of the van alarmed him too. He'd called into the field office for help, guessed at the direction the Mortlock brothers had gone, then climbed in his car and raced after them. As he neared the bottom of the slope, he spotted two cars on the bridge. An ugly sedan was parked sideways, blocking the bridge, and a red minivan had stopped ten feet away. Two men stood in front of the sedan, and an injured woman hugged the side of the bridge. The federal UC agent.

Out of range for radio access, he touched his earpiece and called his supervisor again. "Two cars in a confrontation on Boonville Bridge. I think it's the Mortlocks. An injured young woman is with them as well. I can't see who's in the other vehicle. It could be a transfer. Or maybe a carjacking."

"Is anyone armed?"

"Oh shit. The woman is about to get shot." Grimes pressed the accelerator and raced forward. When he came out of the curve and saw the bridge again, the woman was leaping over the side. The man in gray was on the ground, and the other rushed to him. Was that a prison uniform? It had to be the Mortlocks.

"What's happening?" The voice in his ear had an edge of panic. Grimes had forgotten the phone call was still open.

"One Mortlock is down, and the woman is in the river. The other car is backing away."

"If it's safe to approach, get cuffs on the brothers," his supervisor directed. "If it's not safe, keep eyes on them. Another agent is ten minutes away, coming from the other direction."

"Copy that." At the edge of the bridge, Grimes eased his car to a stop and put it in park. Keeping his eyes on the action, he reached for the binoculars in his glove box, then pulled them to his face to bring the scene up close. The man on the ground was younger, bigger, and looked dead. Shawn Mortlock's freedom had been short-lived. The agent who'd shot him and leapt in the river was a true hero. He hoped she survived. Grimes talked into his earpiece again. "We need a rescue boat and an ambulance for the woman who went over. She shot Shawn Mortlock first though, and I think he's dead."

"Best news I've heard all day." A pause. "Her name is Dallas. She's a UC specialist."

"I'm going in."

"Stay on the line."

Grimes opened his car door and stepped out, but stayed behind it for a moment. The older Mortlock, Aaron, glanced over at him, then stood up. He put his hands in the air, the slump of his shoulders broadcasting defeat.

The other vehicle backed to the end of the bridge, then turned and drove away. Grimes spoke to his boss again. "The people in the other car are leaving. A red minivan. Someone needs to intercept them. We need their statements."

Grimes moved out from behind the door, then strode

quickly toward Mortlock, his weapon out front. The subject gripped something dark. "What do you have? Show it to me nice and slow."

Mortlock held out his hand, palm up, displaying a small device that looked like a miniature remote control.

"What is it?"

"A detonator."

"For a bomb?" Grimes swallowed hard. "Where's the explosive?"

"Taped to the fed in the river."

Oh shit. "Put it on the ground, gently, and step back."

Mortlock did as he was told. Grimes picked up the device, careful to touch only the sides. He couldn't leave it in the road, but he would be glad to turn it over to the bomb squad. For now, he set it on the wall of the bridge.

He cuffed the terrorist without incident, keeping his eye on the downed brother. He wouldn't trust Shawn Mortlock until his body was cold. He locked Aaron in the back of his car, found another pair of cuffs under the seat, and went back for Shawn. The man hadn't moved. Grimes kneeled down, pulled his arms out from under him, and cuffed him behind the back.

He hurried to the bridge wall and scanned the river. The blond agent was dragging herself out of the water about a hundred yards downstream. *Thank god,* she was alive. He touched his earpiece. "Boss, you still there?"

"Yes. What have you got?"

"Dallas is alive and out of the river, so cancel the boat. But she has a bomb strapped to her, and I have the detonator. We need the experts out here ASAP."

"They're already on the way. The Mortlocks have an affinity for explosives, so the incident team at headquarters sent out a bomb unit. They'll be there soon."

Grimes raised his binoculars to look at the woman. Seated on the rocky ground, she hugged her legs to keep warm and was bleeding badly from one shoulder. "One more thing. We need an ambulance. The UC has been shot."

Chapter 40

Saturday, Oct. 11, 2:05 p.m.

Dallas approached the conference room at the field office in DC. Her shoulder was in a sling, but she was taking pain meds and felt pretty damn good. Today, it was simply a joy to be alive. Despite her love for daredevil adventures and risky assignments, she'd come too damn close to death this time. She couldn't wait to get through this meeting, pack her stuff, and get on a plane to Flagstaff in the morning. She planned to take a week or so to rest, visit with her Aunt Lynn, and let Cameron fuss over her. Why not? She couldn't work until her shoulder healed, so she might as well stay medicated and let people pamper her. There was a first time for everything.

When she walked into the meeting, the agents at the table burst into applause. She blushed, another first, and gestured for everyone to stop. The case had turned out pretty well, but not necessarily because of her. She'd lived in the same house as a known criminal and hadn't figured out who he was. And she'd blown her cover by calling her contact on the wrong phone. But there was no need to bring it up. She smiled and moved toward the empty chair.

Drager introduced her to an older man with a turned-down mouth. "This is Special Agent Garrick."

The boss stood and shook her hand. "Good work out

there. Keeping Shawn Mortlock from escaping and committing more acts of terrorism is worthy of a medal."

"Thanks. I was in survival mode for most of the time after Aaron Mortlock drugged me." Dallas sat down. She'd already given a brief statement to an agent at the bridge while she waited for an ambulance, and Drager had visited her for few minutes in the hospital.

"You will be honored for it," Garrick said. "I think it's time you applied for Special Agent status."

She would consider it, but titles didn't mean much to her. She wanted to keep doing work that was interesting and rewarding—and maybe put her language skills to more use. She was seriously tempted to apply to the CIA to take international assignments. But these men didn't need to know that.

Mostly men, anyway. A young Asian woman sat on Drager's other side, and across from her was a middle-aged man with hair implants. She hadn't met either yet, so more introductions followed. Finally, an older woman carrying a can of Mountain Dew came in.

Drager stared at her, then said, "This is Jocelyn Larson, with MPD's homicide division." His voice softened when he said her name.

He had a thing for her. *Sweet.* Dallas nodded at Larson but didn't get up to shake hands. Too much pain and not enough sleep in the noisy hospital. She regretted letting them keep her overnight, but she hadn't wanted to go back to her empty DC apartment, not while feeling that vulnerable. She had put off calling Cameron too, waiting until she felt better.

Drager continued. "Detective Larson is on the team that's investigating both Judge Bidwell's murder and his ex-clerk's. As it turns out, those cases were only marginally connected to the inner circle." He nodded at Detective Larson. "Thanks for coming. Please update everyone on your activities Friday morning."

The detective suppressed a smile. "I went to the judge's house to question his wife, Joan Bidwell, in connection to the clerk's murder. A call had been made from her bank to Callie Sayers, her husband's clerk. But I don't think Joan made the call. I think the judge did." Larson took a drink of her soda. "While I was in the house, I heard Joan implicate the judge in the shooting death of his ex-clerk, then she admitted killing him. Mrs. Bidwell later repeated that confession on video, claiming that she'd snapped. So she'll probably seek an insanity plea."

His own wife had killed him? Stunned, Dallas said, "So Luke Maddox wasn't involved in the judge's death?" She felt a small wave of relief that she'd assessed her target correctly.

"No, but Maddox was at the Bidwell house, seeking closure," the detective explained. "Joan Bidwell confessed to him and admitted to being the anonymous source of the inner circle's funding."

Luke hadn't gone to the senator's house for the home invasion either? A huge wave of relief this time.

Agent Garrick, the supervisor, turned and stared at Detective Larson with his mouth open. "The judge's wife funded the activists?"

"Yes. She felt guilty about her husband's payoffs, and her family partially owns the prisons they were sent to."

Dallas let out an involuntary snort. "I don't think her *snapped* defense will hold up." She turned to Larson. "Did you take Maddox into custody?" He would do time for the acts of sabotage, but not a life sentence for kidnapping and extortion.

"No." The detective and Drager spoke at the same time. Drager added, "Maddox is still at large, but we'll get him."

Dallas kept her face impassive, but she was pleased to know Luke wasn't in custody. Part of her rooted for him to get away. She forced herself to look at Drager and nod. "What about the others?"

Drager grimaced. "Abby Gleeson was shot during the takedown. She drew a weapon on Stella Pearlman." Drager paused, his left eye blinking rapidly. "Cree Songchild, aka Drake Morrison, was arrested and charged. He claims he didn't know Abby had a gun and that Mrs. Pearlman wasn't supposed be there. He also said the senator had child porn on his laptop, and they simply intended to take the laptop and go public with it."

"That's all true," Dallas said, looking around. "But the inner circle also planned to threaten the Pearlmans' dog in exchange for a yes vote on the decriminalization bill." Even though she liked Cree, she couldn't protect him. He'd made his choices. She glanced at Drager. "Did you seize Senator Pearlman's computer?"

"We did, and the underage nude photos were there. Ray Pearlman is in custody too."

She shouldn't care and certainly shouldn't ask, but she did anyway. "What about the legislative vote Friday in the Senate?"

"It failed."

So a bunch of old white men with bottles of scotch in their desks, child porn on their laptops, and mistresses on the side had voted to keep treating potheads like felons. Dallas struggled to keep her face impassive. Luke hadn't even left a legacy of making a difference. She was silent for a long moment. "What else have we got? I know I need to finish my report, but I'm ready to go home."

"The director wants to see you at headquarters on Monday," Drager said. "He's pleased with how you handled the Mortlock brothers."

She hoped to be on a plane home before Monday, and there wasn't much left to say. She already knew Shawn was dead, Aaron was in custody, and the family on the bridge was safe. After dragging herself out of the river, she'd clawed her way up the embankment to the road. By then, three Virginia agents were on the scene. Drager had figured out who Aaron Foster was and guessed at what he had planned, but her contact had been a little too late. She wouldn't say that though. What happened to her wasn't his fault. Infiltrating criminal groups was a risk, and she had taken it willingly.

For another twenty minutes, she shared details of the sabotages she'd participated in and what she'd learned from the inner circle members. The DC team had already searched the farmhouse and confiscated their computers.

"What about Senator Pearlman's campaign funds?" Dallas asked. "Did you track those?"

"The financial team is working on it," Drager said. "But Aaron Mortlock shifted the money to various offshore accounts, and I don't know if we'll ever get it back."

"I guess Pearlman won't need it now." Child pornography charges would keep him from being re-elected. She nodded at Drager. "I'd like to finish my report now and go back to my apartment."

"We're done here anyway." Drager stood. "Thanks, everyone, for coming in. Enjoy the rest of the weekend, and we'll get back to this on Monday." He handed Dallas the laptop that had been sitting in front of him. "We retrieved this from the farmhouse, along with some of your clothes.

They're in the evidence locker."

"Thanks."

Dallas waited while the others filed out of the room. She wanted everyone to go ahead, so she wouldn't have to answer any more questions. As Drager and Larson exited, she overheard him asking the detective to have dinner. Larson squeezed his arm and agreed. Dallas was jealous of their intimacy.

An hour later, she entered her cold quiet DC apartment, feeling both relieved and lonely. But all she had to do was pack, ship a few boxes, and spend one more night here. Tomorrow she would get on a plane and leave. It was time to call Cameron and let him know she was coming home. But Dallas hesitated, knowing she faced a major decision. If she planned to transfer to the CIA, she would have to break up with Cameron. It was only fair. But she wasn't ready for it. She missed him and couldn't imagine walking away again. She also wasn't sure she ever wanted to face death so closely again.

After grabbing a beer from the fridge, she sat down with her laptop and opened the Skype program. With her good arm, she keyed in Dr. Harper's online name and clicked Call. It wasn't right to bother her shrink on Saturday, especially without an appointment or any warning, but she had to talk to her.

A dialogue box opened, and the woman's wrinkled face appeared. Dr. Harper was scowling. "You really need to call me and make an appointment."

"I know. I'm sorry. I've had a rough couple of days."

"I see that." Dr. Harper gestured at the sling. "Tell me what happened."

"I don't want to talk about the assignment."

"What do you want to discuss?"

Why was this so hard? Harper knew all her stupid shortcomings and issues with men. "I don't have my lucky cloth anymore," Dallas said, avoiding the real subject.

"You threw away the last piece?" Dr. Harper beamed with pride. She had orchestrated the cutting and tossing program.

Dallas was tempted to take credit, but couldn't. "Not exactly. I was arrested, and it disappeared when they took my possessions. But I was kind of relieved when I realized it was gone." Dallas felt a lump in her throat. Why did the damn doctor always bring out her emotions? "A few days later, I faced a certain and horrible death, and I survived without my lucky cloth. I didn't even give it a thought. So I think I'm past that whole thing."

"That's wonderful progress." The doctor narrowed her eyes at Dallas. "But that's not why you called, is it?"

She hesitated again. "I had been thinking of joining the CIA, so I could work overseas, travel, and use my language skills."

"And now?"

"I don't know. I'm more worried about undercover assignments now, and I don't want to break up with Cameron."

"Then don't. Give yourself some time to sort it out." Dr. Harper smiled again, the wrinkles around her eyes deepening. "When you're ready, we'll talk about your near-death experience."

"Okay." Dallas didn't think she ever would, but she tried to keep her shrink happy. "I think I'll call Cameron now."

"Is your sex life with him still good?" A deadpan question.

"The best."

"Then don't let him go. The CIA isn't all it's cracked up to be."

Dallas laughed. "Thanks for making time for me."

They both clicked off. Dallas went to the bedroom and dug one of the burner phones from under the bed. She keyed in Cameron's number. She would give their relationship six months with no undercover work and no travel. If she was still happy—and not restless—she'd have her answer.

L.J. Sellers writes the bestselling Detective Jackson mystery/thriller series—a two-time Readers Favorite Award winner—as well as the Agent Dallas series and provocative standalone thrillers. Her 16 novels have been highly praised by reviewers, and she's one of the highest-rated crime fiction authors on Amazon.

Detective Jackson Mysteries:

    The Sex Club
    Secrets to Die For
    Thrilled to Death
    Passions of the Dead
    Dying for Justice
    Liars, Cheaters & Thieves
    Rules of Crime
    Crimes of Memory
    Deadly Bonds
    Wrongful Death

Agent Dallas Thrillers:

    The Trigger
    The Target
    The Trap

Standalone Thrillers:

    The Baby Thief
    The Gauntlet Assassin
    The Lethal Effect

L.J. resides in Eugene, Oregon where many of her novels are set and is an award-winning journalist who earned the Grand

Neal. She's also the founder of Housing Help, a charity dedicated to keeping families from becoming homeless. When not plotting murders or working with her foundation, she enjoys standup comedy, cycling, social networking, and attending mystery conferences. She's also been known to jump out of airplanes..

Thanks for reading my novel. If you enjoyed it, please leave a review or rating online. Find out more about my work at ljsellers.com, where you can sign up to hear about new releases. —L.J.